# Bad Blood in Kansas

John Carshalton, late of the British Army, returns to the town of Arabella in Kansas to take up a new job as town sheriff. He quickly earns the respect of the townspeople and enjoys a peaceful life until he gets word of outlaw gangs terrorizing towns along the Kansas–Missouri border. US Army intelligence suggests that these are no ordinary gangs, but part of a larger, more sinister force, and when John is asked by an army officer to pose as a deserter from the British Army in Canada and try to infiltrate whatever kind of force is being raised, he agrees, believing this to be a simple fact-finding mission. However, John soon finds him caught up in a web of violence and intrigue that threatens to destroy him and all he holds dear.

# Bad Blood in Kansas

Tom R. Wade

**A Black Horse Western**

ROBERT HALE

© Tom R. Wade 2017
First published in Great Britain 2017


ISBN 978-0-7198-2489-0


The Crowood Press
The Stable Block
Crowood Lane
Ramsbury
Marlborough
Wiltshire SN8 2HR

www.bhwesterns.com

Robert Hale is an imprint
of The Crowood Press


The right of Tom R. Wade to be identified as
author of this work has been asserted by him
in accordance with the Copyright, Designs and
Patents Act 1988

Typeset by
Derek Doyle & Associates, Shaw Heath
Printed and bound in Great Britain by
CPI Group (UK) Ltd, Croydon, CR0 4YY

# CHAPTER ONE

Isaac Townsend would never be sure how long the lone rider had sat at the top of the hill watching him plough.

It was mid-afternoon and he was ploughing the last piece of land he owned that was not already being used for crops. He needed every piece of arable that he could find, but this ground was stubborn and unyielding and the muscles of his back strained as he fought to help the big horses drag the plough through the hard ground. His head was down, eyes staring at the dust as he drove forward.

Something made him look up and there the man sat watching him with amusement. Isaac took in at once the dull grey of the man's uniform, the red sash around the waist, the battered kepi pushed back on his head. The man raised the cap in mock salute and then threw back his head and let out an animal-like shriek. This was answered at once by dozens more voices. The man galloped forward, past Isaac and down towards the bottom of the field.

Immediately he saw the other riders flitting through the trees at the bottom of the field he knew that there was danger. He struggled out of the leather straps that fixed him to the horse and plough and began to run down the field towards his small farmhouse. He stumbled and fell at one point and a sharp stone tore through the leg of his breeches and gashed his knee. He vaguely thought, 'Annie will give me hell for that.'

He ran through the trees at the bottom of the field and then he could see his cabin and barn at the top of the rise. He could see wisps of smoke from the back of the house and the barn was ablaze.

'Annie!' he shouted as he rushed up the hill towards the cabin.

She appeared from the back of the cabin, her blonde hair darkened by smoke and her face smeared with soot and grime. She was coughing heavily. He ran to her and pulled her up in his arms.

'I saved the house, Isaac,' she croaked. 'I saved the house. We lost the barn. I got the cow out but we lost the barn.'

Tears were streaking through the soot now. He held her to him, soothing and gentle as she sobbed against him. He fought his own tears as he watched the big barn he had been so proud of burn. He remembered the warm spring day the neighbours had come to help him build it. Trestle tables laid out with food and beer. Old Perry Connor sawing away on his fiddle. He remembered thinking he had probably never been so happy in all his life.

She pulled back slightly and looked up at him. 'They were Rebs, Isaac. They were Johnny Rebs. That don't make no sense.'

He looked past her over to the distant shape of the town. He could already see smoke and flames rising. He even fancied he heard gunshots and screams.

He looked down at her. 'No, Annie, it don't.'

No sense whatsoever, he thought. He had believed he had done enough; fought hard enough for the Union cause, and helped to defeat the enemy in a war that had finished six years before.

He stood helplessly, feeling lost.

'No, Annie, it don't make no sense whatever.'

# CHAPTER TWO

Josh Ramsey sat and watched the cloud of dust from the buckboard getting closer. He felt relaxed and at peace. The heat of the day was beginning to fade and he was enjoying the slight cool that was creeping into the air.

Around him the small Kansas town of Arabella bustled.

A year ago, bustle was not a word you would have applied to Arabella, but that was before the shoot-out.

The town had been forgotten and passed by in the rush west, but everything changed when a young English army captain misguidedly went absent without leave from his regiment in Canada having killed a man in a duel. That Englishman, heading west through Kansas, stepped in to save an old lawman who was in a fix, and in doing so made a friend who stood with him when the dead man's brother, a hired assassin and a group of outlaws combined to put the town in danger.

What happened was a shoot-out, the result of which being that suddenly everybody knew where Arabella was and quite a few wanted to go there. Arabella had notoriety.

Now the cause of it all, John Carshalton, was coming home.

After the gunfight John had decided to go back to Canada and face the music. He took with him Connie Brady, a saloon girl who had fallen madly in love with him, and it had taken near death to make John realize that he felt just the same about her. He had taken her back to be married, although what his wealthy English parents and the British Army had made of Connie, Josh could only imagine.

He could see the two of them, still blurred by the slight heat haze and the small cloud of dust being raised by the wheels of the buggy.

All Josh did know was that the court martial that John had attended had ended better that anybody would have thought and he was given an honourable discharge from the army; indeed he could have retained his commission. Also the marriage had gone ahead, and those two facts were all Josh needed to know at this stage.

He lost sight of the buggy for a moment as it disappeared behind the buildings at the edge of town and then moments later reappeared trotting down Main Street towards the sheriff's office and jailhouse. Josh rose to his feet and stepped to the edge

9

of the sidewalk.

John pulled the horses to a stop and grinned up at Josh. The familiar boyish good looks were still there, marred only by a small scar on his face from over-exuberant use of a sabre in training and a missing ear lobe taken away by a shot from a duelling pistol on this very street.

'About time,' was Josh's gruff greeting to John.

John beamed back. 'And a very good day to you, Deputy Sheriff Ramsey. I trust we find you in good health, old chap.'

Josh's eyes fell on Connie, who smiled warmly back at him. She was just the same, soft and pretty with long black hair and dark eyes. Josh had always had a soft spot for Connie and she forced the first smile from him.

'Well, Mrs. Carshalton, I do declare that marriage agrees with you. Damn it if you are not prettier than ever . . .'

Connie blushed and Josh wondered how long it had been since he had been able to make a saloon girl blush, then figured that he had probably never been able to do it. In any case this girl was no longer a saloon girl.

John was gazing around him in amazement. From where he sat he could see what were clearly a hotel, a bank, a schoolhouse and the beginnings of a church.

'Josh, what has happened to Arabella?'

'Well, to start with, you happened to it, a gunfight

10

happened to it and then Mr Declan Finn happened to it.'

'Declan Finn?'

'Mr Finn is what is known these days as a businessman. Back in my day we might have called him something else.'

'You sound as though you don't approve of Mr Finn?'

'Ain't for me to approve or disapprove. He don't break any laws and the town is benefitting from what he is doing. We now have a bank, a hotel, and the church and schoolhouse are near done. Don't you worry none, John, you'll meet Finn soon enough.'

'I was surprised enough when you said we had a hotel. Did you book us into it?'

'Nope.'

'Why, pray?'

'Mr Finn would not accept your booking. The reason Mr Finn would not accept your booking is that Mr Finn has built you a house.'

'He has what?'

'Mr Finn did not think that the man who is becoming our town sheriff should live in the hotel. So then, he had a house built.'

Connie's face had lit up at the mention of a house, but now she was expressionless, watching John carefully to see what his reaction would be.

'We will book into the hotel and then I will speak with Mr Finn.'

John was aware that Connie's face had fallen

11

slightly but when he looked over at her she just smiled encouragingly. He turned back to Josh.

'Do you think you can arrange a meeting?'

'I sure can. Declan Finn is like a prairie dog on heat to meet you.'

'Why?'

'Declan Finn is a careful man. He wants to do business in this town and he wants anybody he thinks is important on his side. Hell, he's even buying me drinks and I'm retiring.' He looked anxiously at John. 'I am retiring, right?'

John looked surprised. 'I'm sorry to hear that.'

Josh looked set to explode. 'Damn you, John. It was all agreed. You are taking over as sheriff. I'm stepping down.'

John smiled serenely. 'And so it is, my quick-tempered friend. I just wanted to test that you are as gullible as always.'

Josh snarled, 'One of these days,' and then broke into a broad grin. 'Damn I've missed you, you arrogant English . . .' He suddenly became aware of Connie. 'Sorry, ma'am.'

Connie broke into giggles. 'Josh, did you just "ma'am" me? Nobody worried about cussing in front of me when I worked at the Drovers' Rest.'

'Yeah, well you don't work at the Drovers any more. You are a respectable married woman and you are either ma'am or Mrs. Carshalton, and if any of those bar flies get confused over that let me know and I'll straighten them out.'

Connie jumped down from the buggy, rushed to Josh and threw her arms around him, kissing him on the cheek. 'Oh Josh, it is so good to be back.'

Josh hugged her back, awkwardly at first and then tightly. 'And it's good to have you back, both of you. Now go and get checked in to Arabella's classy new hotel and I will let Finn know you're here.'

Alexander Julius Hannibal Fairweather III enjoyed a good flogging. That is to say that he enjoyed seeing them administered to others. He had no desire to feel the bite of the lash on his own skin.

However, sitting in his favourite chair in the middle of the parade ground watching as a soldier, stripped to the waist, twisted and turned and cried out at each crack of the whip was Fairweather's idea of an afternoon well spent.

Fairweather was only 33 years old but the narrow pinched face and protruding chin aged him. He smiled little, but this afternoon he did allow himself a broad grin, made broader by the fact that Regimental Sergeant Major Breeze stood a few feet away and hated every moment of the punishment that was being dealt out to one of his men.

'You have no stomach for this I suspect, Breeze.' The slow Southern drawl seemed to emphasize the contempt in his voice.

Breeze took a deep breath and controlled his anger. 'I have stomach for most things, General, but I can't abide a flogging.'

13

'Can you not? Well stop your men from stealing and you will see the lash used no more.'

'We had been on patrol, sir. He went to the mess to see if there was food, and there was.'

'Understand this, Sergeant Major Breeze. The men will eat when I tell them to eat. They will drink when I tell them to drink, and they will defecate when I tell them they can. Is that understood?'

'I think you have made the point, General.'

'Hmmm, do you, do you now?' He made a steeple of his fingers and stared thoughtfully at the punishment being administered by a less than enthusiastic corporal.

He paused long enough for a couple more lashes to be applied and then as though having finally solved a great problem waved his hand at the corporal, who stepped away with obvious relief and let the victim sag unconscious in his chains.

Breeze stood motionless, staring ahead, his face expressionless. He had had many officers he disliked over the years, but not one he disliked as intensely as General Alexander Fairweather, head of the New Army of Northern Virginia.

Fairweather was born into a rich Southern family with a long tradition of military glory behind them, a tradition that the family boasted stretched back to Agincourt and beyond. He had grown up learning of the great warriors of the ancient world that had supplied his names and those of his father and grandfather.

His most precious toys had been his hobby horse and his wooden sword, the latter used liberally to beat the Negro children who were forced to play with him. His place in the army was a foregone conclusion and he duly attended West Point Military Academy.

However, on the eve of his graduation Virginia seceded from the Union and he went home immediately to take up arms to fight for the freedom of the South.

His war however, did not work out as he planned. He was made a lieutenant but he proved to be an unpopular officer with his men and he constantly found himself sent to command details guarding supply trains, and even for a time the military prison at Andersonville where he could, at least, give expression to his natural cruelty.

Shortage of officers meant he could not be kept from the front line forever and he found himself in July 1864 at that bloodbath, outstanding even after so many bloodbaths, which became known within the three-day battle of Gettysburg as The Wheat Field.

That innocent-looking field of swaying wheat ready for harvest became a place of bloody slaughter, of attack and counter-attack, until at last the impatient Alexander was given the order to lead his company as part of what the Confederate generals believed, quite wrongly, would be the final assault that would drive the Yankees from the field.

15

This was what the young lieutenant had been waiting for all his life. Now at last was his chance to add himself to the long line of heroes, to be able to tell grandchildren his own tales of derring-do.

It vexed Fairweather later that he could never quite remember what the rallying cry was that he gave his men before they moved forward. He hoped it was 'Follow me, men, through hell and out the other side,' but he was plagued with an awful doubt that he might have thought of that heroic challenge later.

Whatever the cry had been, as he rushed forward his men rushed after him. Whilst they, in common with almost every other soldier he had ever commanded, hated him deeply, they were forced to admit he was doing the one thing he was asked to do and that was to lead from the front.

With a mighty rebel yell they surged forward behind their officer.

At this moment Fairweather realized that he had failed to draw his sword. To try to stop and do it would have been to have his men brought to a halt behind him, so he had no choice but to draw it as he ran, and immediately sliced it deeply through his leg just above the knee. With a scream he fell.

His men would have naturally assumed that he had taken a Yankee musket ball and continued on, many of them trampling over their fallen leader, whether by accident or design nobody would ever know. The Confederate soldiers rushed on into hell but without Alexander Fairweather III to lead them out the other side most of them died in that open space already liberally covered with corpses.

Fairweather recovered consciousness to find himself alone in the dark and weak from loss of blood. He crawled, confused, in what he hoped was the direction of the Confederate position but found himself surrounded by a Union patrol and was taken to an exhausted field surgeon already standing next to a pile of amputated limbs, to which Lieutenant Alexander Fairweather's festering lower leg was quickly added.

Fairweather spent the remainder of the war in the Federal Army prison in Chicago. He now had the time to feel a great sense of grievance at being abandoned, as he believed, by his own army and a festering hatred for the Federal government at the appalling treatment he received in the prison. The irony of the latter complaint was lost on him.

But now at last, sitting in his own army camp in the thin sunshine of Missouri, Alexander Fairweather III felt that his chance was coming to change the course of history. He smoothed down his uniform, admiring the crisp lines of the grey tunic and pants; even the careful fold of the right leg of the pants just above the missing knee looked fine and military.

The pleasure of the flogging had put him in good humour even with the taciturn Breeze.

'I have congratulated Captain White on the

success of the last mission, Breeze, and he was gen-
erous in his praise of you and the men.'

Breeze's face hardened. Praise from a sewer rat
like White was no praise at all as far as he was concerned. Fairweather was chatting cheerfully on.

'You stirred up a hornet's nest and then swatted
them. You have sent a clear message of our intent
without, at this stage, any great loss of life. I think
the farmers and the store owners know we are here.'

'The men did well, General,' Breeze said with
only a touch of sullenness, and he looked pointedly
at the now empty post where blood could be seen
soaking into the dust.

Fairweather wondered whether to react to this
hint of insolence but decided to take the words at
face value and continued to admire his uniform
instead.

Of course, he thought, he was young to be a
general in peacetime but then when you can choose
your own rank all things are possible, and in any
case, he reasoned, it would not be peacetime for
long.

Josh's description of the Arabella Central Hotel was
no exaggeration. John and Connie entered a lobby
area with soft carpet on the floor and leather chairs
set around low polished tables. The windows were
curtained and potted plants stood around. It was a
far cry from the Drovers' Rest Saloon and Boarding
House, the hospitality of which could best be

described as 'basic'.

The desk clerk, on hearing John's name, immediately discovered that the only room unoccupied was the Bridal Suite, which of course would, by way of apology for the inconvenience, be let at the same rate as a standard room. John doubted any of this was true but was becoming too tired from the journey to care, and besides, he had disappointed Connie once already today and decided this time just to enjoy her excited expression. He allowed the bellhop to gather the bags and lead them up the wide carpeted stairs to a room so well appointed that Connie could not suppress a small squeal of delight.

As Connie began to unpack, John sat in a chair by the window and gazed down the main street at the new businesses that were beginning to spring up.

The old general store was still there. It was there that he had been given a box room at the back to sleep in, in return for helping in the shop. In that box room, he had read *The Pickwick Papers* to Connie by candlelight after she had finished her duties at the saloon, and Connie had fallen in love with the quietly spoken Englishman, burdened as he was by duty and guilt.

After some thirty minutes the bellhop was back with a message that Mr Declan Finn would be honoured to receive Mr and Mrs Carshalton in his office for some light refreshment.

Declan Finn's office was just behind the lobby

and was every bit as grand as the rest of the hotel. Josh was already there, sprawled in one of the comfortable armchairs. Declan Finn sat behind a large leather-topped desk, and both men rose as John and Connie entered.

John had expected to see a mature man and was surprised see that Declan was in his twenties and therefore not much older than himself. He was shorter than John and already beginning to show some paunch around the middle but the face was youthful and handsome and the smile broad and welcoming. He advanced around the desk. 'John Carshalton, I presume.'

They shook hands, both bowing slightly, with a firm 'How do you do.' John turned to bring Connie forward. 'May I present my wife, Concepta.'

Declan bowed deeply, taking Connie's hand and bringing to his lips. 'Mrs. Carshalton, welcome.' He straightened but retained her hand a little longer. 'Our friend Mr Ramsey is a fine lawman but when it comes to describing you he has not come close to doing justice to your beauty.'

Connie smiled at Declan and John could see the slight hardening of her eyes. If Declan wanted to impress Connie, flowery praise was not the way to do it.

'Would that be a Limerick accent I hear there, Declan?'

Declan laughed, 'Indeed it would, madam, indeed it would, and a fine Irish girl yourself I hear.'

'Long ago, Mr Finn. I like to think of myself as an American now.'

'As indeed do we all, Mrs. Carshalton. Now please, would you join me in a little light refreshment?'

They sat around a small table on which were tea and a plate covered in small delicate pastries beside which stood a large decanter of Madeira wine.

When all this had been dispensed and the niceties observed John asked the question he had been longing to ask from the moment he had shaken hands with the Irishman.

'Forgive my directness, Mr Finn . . .'

'Declan, please. I feel we are all going to be friends here.' John exchanged a glance with Josh, who was chewing suspiciously on a pastry, trying to decide what was in it.

'Forgive my directness, Declan, but what line of business are you in?'

'More than one, Sheriff.'

'I fear you are a little premature, Declan. I am not yet sheriff of Arabella.'

'But surely it is a mere formality?'

'That's what I keep telling him,' Josh interrupted through a mouthful of pastry. 'He's riding to Abilene day after tomorrow to be sworn in. I was only a deputy, of course, but John here being a hero and a fearsome man with a revolver gets to be a full-blown sheriff.'

Declan looked around uncertainly at this but

there was a twinkle in the eye of the old lawman and John laughed.

'I am a married man, Josh. I need all the money I can get.'

Declan beamed at them, 'And may I be one of the first in Arabella to congratulate you. And you, Mrs. Carshalton. Now, do you find the room to your liking?'

Connie smiled, 'Very comfortable indeed.'

John leaned forward. 'I was saying, Declan, that I am curious as to what business you are involved in.'

Declan reluctantly took his eyes off Connie and turned back to John.

'Of course you are. You will already have found the town much changed and I will admit that I have made my modest contribution to the changes. You see, Sheriff . . .'

John waved his hand. 'John will suffice for the present.'

'As you will. You see, John, after the events that occurred so many months ago, Arabella acquired a certain notoriety. Would you not agree, Josh?'

Josh was caught by surprise lifting another pastry to his mouth, having given up trying to identify what was inside but deciding they tasted well enough.

'Damn right – sorry Connie – after news of the shoot-out got around they came pouring in from the east thicker than flies on a dead buffalo.'

'As Josh so colourfully describes. Arabella quickly became what could best be described as a tourist attraction. Naturally as a man with an eye for business I could see that this town needed a good hotel, no disrespect to the establishment already in operation.'

Josh stopped for a moment between pastries to snort derisively. 'Even the cockroaches wouldn't stay at the Drovers'.'

'However,' Declan continued 'once I had built this I knew that the notoriety of the shoot-out would not last indefinitely and I would need other types of customers to serve. There were two – one, the hunting parties from the east going west to where the buffalo is plentiful. Not only am I giving them a place to stay en route, I have engaged the services of well-known buffalo hunters and organize and supply the hunting parties. Secondly, we have businessmen.'

John raised an eyebrow. 'I was not aware there was much business to be done in Arabella.'

'One word, John – grain.'

'Grain?'

'Kansas is fast establishing itself as a farming state. Farmers want to sell grain. I want to buy it and sell it on. I am planning a number of large grain stores just on the edge of town. If I can move sufficient quantities I may be able to interest the railroad in laying a spur line out here with all the attendant prosperity that would bring.'

Josh had finally hit his pastry quota and was busily washing them down with fine Madeira. 'What

Declan means is prosperity for him.'

Declan smiled, 'As you can tell, Josh does not much like me.'

'Ain't a matter of liking, Declan, I like you well enough, it's just that I don't trust you. I have this feeling that one night I am going to go to sleep in Arabella and wake up in Finnville.'

'And there you are wrong, my friend. My mother, God rest her soul, was always known as Bella. A fine name for a fine woman, so one of the things that attracted me to this town was the name. Arabella will always be Arabella while I am here.'

He turned to John, who was digesting the information given.

'Now John, perhaps you can answer a question for me.'

John nodded. 'I'll try.'

'Honoured as I am to have you staying in my hotel – and please let me know if there is anything I can do to make your stay more comfortable – I will own to a small disappointment that you and your lovely wife are not enjoying the intimacy of your own home. I had dearly hoped it would be to your liking.'

'Declan, as I am constantly being reminded I am about to become sheriff of Arabella. Therefore, I will represent the law in this town. The law cannot be partial. I cannot do the job I am paid to do if I am beholden to an important local businessman.'

Declan bowed his head slightly to acknowledge

the small piece of flattery.

'However,' John continued, 'I have been giving it some thought. If you would be so kind as to advise me of all the costs incurred in the construction of the property. My father is still in Canada doing business. I will send a message to him asking him to loan me the sum required. My father is many miles away and my opportunity to show any bias towards him is unlikely. As soon as I have reimbursed you for your costs I will be delighted to use the house as you generously intended. Does this meet with your approval, sir?'

Declan leaned back in his chair and held up his hands palms outward in mock surrender.

'You are a man who knows his own mind, John, indeed you are. I must reluctantly accept and, of course, wish you both every happiness.'

He held his hand out to John, who rose to accept it with another formal bow.

# CHAPTER THREE

After the meeting with Declan Finn John felt a little easier in his mind. He, like Josh, did not wholly trust Declan but everything he was doing seemed legitimate.

The money from his father arrived quickly so he could square things with Declan and move Connie into the new house.

He was duly sworn in as planned and was now officially sheriff of Arabella.

From there things settled to a routine. John dealt with minor disagreements and domestic upsets but otherwise he patrolled, read the handbills that came down from Abilene and familiarized himself with the contents of the gun cabinet, many of which were new to him.

Sometimes, of course, the mundane could become significant without you realizing it.

One evening John was sitting sifting through paperwork and telling himself that in another hour he would be heading back for some home cooking, when Sam from the saloon sent over a message that three young men were refusing to hand over their guns as per the house rules laid down by John.

The three young men in question were all English; Gerald Bromyard-Finch, Thomas Bruce and Lord Frederick Malvern. The three old school friends, now all Oxford graduates, were whiling away the time by conquering the west, before they stepped into the roles back in England that their fathers had chosen for them.

They had decided to do this one step at a time, and the first step was to travel on one of Declan Finn's buffalo shoots; having killed almost every breed of creature in England and Scotland they could now assist in decimating the big lumbering creatures that had helped to sustain the way of life for the Indian tribes for thousands of years.

Determined to look the part they had all purchased Colt revolvers complete with holsters, and felt ready to tame the west. It came as a disappointment then to find that they could not even tame a barkeeper with bad teeth into letting them wear their expensive side arms in his saloon.

Wearily John strapped on his gun belt and crossed the street to the saloon.

He spotted the problem as soon as he walked in through the swing doors. The young men were leaning arrogantly against the bar and John could hear the English public-school accents as he approached. He stopped in front of Gerald, whom he correctly decided looked most like the leader. As well as the pistols, all three had dressed as they fondly believed western heroes dressed although, as anybody could have told them, only in the books sold in dime stores in New York.

Gerald greeted John with an insolent grin.

'Well, well, is this a real-life sheriff I see before me? Are you a real-life sheriff?'

'So they tell me. Now I need you to hand your guns over the bar or leave.'

'Well bless my soul. An Englishman. You are an Englishman?' Gerald seemed to feel the need to question his own statements of fact.

'No, I am a sheriff and I am asking you to hand over your guns.'

The two young men behind Gerald stirred uneasily and began to look nervous.

'Look Gerald, perhaps we ought to go along with this. We do not want trouble with the law.'

Gerald ignored them. 'I'm sorry, old boy, I am a little confused. You sound like an Englishman and yet you maintain that you are not. Yet, upon my soul, you even sound like a gentleman. Are you a gentleman?'

Lord Frederick attempted to defuse what he could see was fast becoming a bad situation.

'What he is saying, Gerald, is that it is neither here nor there if he is English or if he is a gentleman. He is the law and perhaps we should just jolly well respect that and do as he asks.'

Gerald spun round to face his two companions. 'What is the matter with you fellows? I have not come thousands of miles to be pushed around by a barman and a chap who cannot make his mind up which country he comes from.'

John felt his patience ebbing away. At school he had been in the boxing ring with enough Geralds to know the type. Always so entitled, born in to a world of privilege.

Sneering references to his father as 'trade' – the English love of money inherited as opposed to money earned.

'I am asking you just once more.'

Gerald's sneer threatened to engulf his face. 'My dear chap, I do not think you appreciate who you are talking to.'

'Possibly not, but I know *what* I am talking to. Just one more bored lout running out of ways to spend his allowance.'

'You are damned impertinent, sir. I will not bandy words with some jumped-up down-on-his-luck, probably chucked out of some third-grade school and fetching up here as the local peeler. Am I right, eh what?'

He turned round to beam at his friends, both of whom refused to be impressed by his bad behaviour.

John's patience now finished ebbing and vanished completely. He stepped forward and deftly lifted the pistol from Gerald's holster. Holding it around the barrel he brought the gun straight down with some force, catching Gerald's nose on the way. Gerald went down holding his nose, which was now spurting blood.

Gerald leaned back against the footrail and looked up piteously. 'You bloke ma doud, you absoloot rutter.'

The other two young men were quickly unbuckling their gun belts as John hauled Gerald to his feet. The young man was still trying to stem the flow of blood from his nose.

Frederick stepped forward. 'Look, Sheriff, may I apologize for my friend. He really is a thoroughly decent fellow but we had a few brandies with the Irish chappie and I fear we overindulged a little. Gerald has never been the best at holding his drink.'

There was a muffled 'I thay' from Gerald but they all ignored him.

John turned to the barman. 'Sam. Get these gentlemen a drink on my account.'

Frederick beamed with relief. 'That is thoroughly decent of you, Sheriff.'

John smiled. 'We are thoroughly decent people in Arabella. Is that not right, Sam?'

Sam treated them all to a gap-toothed grin. 'Damn right we are, Sheriff, and I will blow the brains out of anybody who says different.'

John turned to leave but Sam called him to one side. 'Actually, Sheriff, you don't have a slate here any more.'

'Why not, pray?'

'You know Mr Declan Finn bought the Drovers' two days ago.'

Indeed John did, it had been the talk of the town. Rumours abounded that Finn planned an upmarket brothel and casino. John doubted it. Finn was, he felt, subtler than that, but time would tell.

'And he says that your money ain't no good here. Anything you want is on the house.'

John sighed, 'Tell Mr Finn that it is very kind of him but my money is good here and I would appreciate my slate being reinstated.'

He beamed at the sullen Gerald and his two companions and walked out into the night.


The first realization Sheriff Theodore MacFarlane had that he was not going to enjoy the quiet evening he had planned was the moment a cannonball came through the window of his office, destroyed the desk he had been sitting at a few minutes before, went through the wall behind it and partly stove in the bars to one of the cells.

MacFarlane, having finished his work for the evening, had moved over to his rocking chair by the stove with a jug of beer and one of the latest dime novels brought in on the stage from back east. MacFarlane had little time for the novels depicting life in the Wild West, which he considered ridiculous, living as he was a few miles inside the Kansas border from Missouri and enjoying, up until this moment, a peaceful life.

MacFarlane favoured a series of novels concerning explorers in Africa. The sheriff had only a notion of where Africa might be, but full as it was of jungles, ferocious animals and bloodthirsty savages, MacFarlane considered it must be 'one hell of a place'.

As the cannonball passed through, MacFarlane was engulfed in a cloud of brick dust. Half blinded, he grabbed a rifle from the rack and staggered out into the street. The sight that greeted him was his idea of what hell might look like on a bad day.

Many buildings were on fire and there was screaming and shouting all around him. The street was full of horses, and on the horses were men in the uniform of the defeated Confederate army.

As he struggled to make sense of what he was seeing a rifle butt caught him just behind his left ear and he had a vague image of the hitching rail outside his office coming up to meet his face, and then blackness.

When he opened his eyes again it was see his deputy Evan Williams leaning over him. 'Are you OK, Sheriff?'

MacFarlane considered this for a moment, said 'no' and then turned to one side to vomit in the dust.

When he had finished Williams helped him to his feet. He leaned heavily on the hitching rail to keep himself upright and surveyed the scene of devastation around him.

Williams made to take hold of his arm again but MacFarlane impatiently waved him away.

'They was Rebs, Sheriff. What's going on?'

All MacFarlane could manage, with great sincerity, was 'Hell if I know.'

John was trying to convince himself that he was enjoying life as the sheriff of Arabella but he was not entirely succeeding. He had returned to his office on the night that he had taken the guns from the English buffalo hunters, angry with himself. He had used excessive force when it was not needed. He partly knew why. The three young men were a reminder of England and by that a reminder of his time in the army, when he had worn the uniform of Her Imperial Majesty Queen Victoria with enormous pride.

He knew the anger against these young men was unreasonable. Was he any better than them? Cabling his father for money so that he could salve his conscience against obvious bribery and please his pretty bride.

He knew he had much to be thankful for. He loved his life with Connie and he was in a town where people liked and respected him. He was frustrated by his own ability to enjoy what he had.

He saw the wagon trains heading west full of people trying to escape tyranny or famine, huddled on their wagons with all their possessions in the world strapped on the back. He could get what he wanted by asking his rich parents for help.

He brooded over it for several days. Connie knew that something was wrong but knew also that she must give him his own time to tell her what it was.

Finally sitting on his own porch listening to Connie singing happily to herself as she worked he had resolved to come to terms with his new life and enjoy it for what it was.

It was at that precise moment that Josh crossed the street to impart some news to him.

'There's an army colonel in your office waiting to talk to you.'

# CHAPTER FOUR

When John entered his office he was unsure what to expect.

'Army colonel' did not define which army. He had a sinking feeling in his stomach that he was about to be confronted by a red-coated British Army officer explaining to him that he needed to return to Canada to answer more questions.

He was relieved to find instead a US Army colonel. He wore the slightly longer fatigue blouse that distinguished him from the US Cavalry. This man, John decided, was probably infantry, but it was hard to tell with the relaxed style of dress of many in the US military since the war. The man was, John thought with a touch of snobbishness, by American standards downright dapper.

The colonel was small in stature with a neatly trimmed moustache and smartly parted hair that stopped just above his collar. He was sitting in front of John's desk drinking coffee from a chipped tin mug. He smiled and rose as John entered and extended his hand.

'Sheriff John Carshalton, I presume?'

John took the offered hand and bowed slightly. 'Your servant, sir.'

'How do you do, Sheriff. May I introduce myself? I am Colonel Reynolds, currently stationed at Fort Macey in Missouri.' He looked apologetically at the cup in his hand. 'Forgive me, but your deputy told me to go ahead and help myself.'

John was about to explain that Josh was not his deputy but just someone who now, finding himself with nothing to do, spent more time in the office than he had when he was deputy.

'Not at all. Please be seated, Colonel.'

John poured himself a cup of coffee from the pot on the stove and dropped into his chair behind the desk. 'Now, Colonel, how can I help you?'

'I will come straight to the point. We, that is the US Army, need your help.'

'I? I am at a loss to imagine what possible help I could give the US Army.'

'Have you heard of the raids that have been occurring near the Kansas–Missouri border?'

'A little. I assume them to be the work of the James gang or whatever other band of outlaws have formed since the war.'

Reynolds took a loud gulp from his coffee mug. 'So did we, right up until they started using artillery.'

36

'Artillery, as in cannons?'

'The very same.'

John thought for a moment. 'Well, it is unusual, I will allow, but not impossible that some of these outlaws have laid their hands on some old army surplus.'

'Men who rob banks and trains, rob banks and trains. They do not destroy property, shoot up towns and then ride away without a cent to show for it. No, whoever is responsible for this wants to terrorize the population.'

'And do you have any idea who that might be?'

'That, Captain Carshalton, is where you come in.'

At the mention of 'Captain' John frowned.

'I think you will find, sir, that the jurisdiction of a small-town sheriff does not stretch over the border to Missouri or indeed much beyond the outskirts of this very town.'

Reynolds treated John to what he probably believed was a warm smile. 'Granted, but a British Army deserter on the other hand could probably travel quite freely.'

John put the coffee cup down on the desk with more force than he intended and some of the contents splashed over.

'I think, sir, you have been misinformed. Yes, I was subject to a court martial but I was cleared of all charges and could have retained my commission. As it was I chose an honourable discharge.'

Reynolds raised his hand. 'I am quite aware of

that, Captain Carshalton. Indeed, in my communi-
cations with your colonel he praised you highly and
expressed his regret that you had chosen to leave
the service.'

'Well then. . . ?'

'What I am hoping is that whoever is behind this
does not know that.'

'But you do not know who that is?'

'No.' Colonel Reynolds suddenly seemed weary.
He drank some more coffee and cleared his throat.
'This, Captain Carshalton, is what we do know.
There have been several raids on towns and farms
close to the Missouri border. The raids have
involved cavalry, infantry and in some cases a small
amount of artillery. Rumours abound that somebody is looking for ex-Confederate soldiers,
mercenaries and even deserters from other armies.
Normally I would ask for reinforcements and comb
all of Missouri until we found them – however, there
has been a great deal of movement amongst the
Indian nations, which has pulled many troops
further west. Frankly, Captain, I am badly stretched
at present. I need to locate this,' he paused as if
searching for the right word, '"army" and put paid
to this nonsense as swiftly as possible.'

'And you think I can do that for you?'

'It is a known fact that you went absent without
leave from the British Army. What happened since is
probably less well known. We want you to pose as a
deserter, locate the person or persons behind all

this and lead us to him. It is a simple reconnaissance mission.'

Reynolds went back to draining his coffee cup and without waiting to be asked stood up and went to the stove to refill his mug. John sat staring past the colonel, trying to clear his head.

'I have duties and responsibilities here.'

'You have a deputy.'

'Josh is no longer a deputy.'

'Nonetheless, I would presume that he could take over the responsibility for a short while, and I assure you, Captain, I see this matter being resolved within just a few days.'

John sighed. Everything in him was telling him to flatly refuse and get back to his job, but something else was in conflict with this good sense and he did not want to admit to himself what it was.

'I will give it some thought, sir.'

'Very well, but I must press you for an early decision. I am staying at the hotel and I will await your visit.'

General Fairweather was reading a book on the life of Alexander the Great when the flap of his tent was moved aside and Captain Frank White entered. Fairweather sighed and put the book to one side.

'What is it, White?'

'I need to speak with you, sir.'

'And remarkably that is just what you are doing.'

Fairweather could not bring himself to like

White. He was, he felt, an uncouth lout and was surprised that he had reached the rank of captain in the Confederate army, even in time of war. At best he wore an approximation of a captain's uniform. His hair was always greasy and far too long. Indeed, personal hygiene never seemed a matter of any importance to him. He had perpetual stubble that never seemed to grow into a beard.

'What did you want to speak with me about?'

If Fairweather had known the truth about White he would have liked him considerably less. White had been a private in the 15th South Carolina Infantry and had seen the war simply as a means of looting bodies, Union or Confederate, for whatever he could. When he had seen that the battle of Gettysburg was going badly for the South he had stripped off as much of his uniform as he could and tried to escape. Seeing that this was impossible he stole the uniform of a dead Confederate captain and it was in this that he was captured and sent eventually to the same prison camp as Fairweather. Quickly identifying Fairweather as rich, White had cultivated his friendship, although when Fairweather returned to his family plantation and found his home destroyed and his slaves gone White decided that he might be better on his own. He attached himself to one after another of the bands of disaffected rebels busily robbing trains and banks. White was always on the move, always avoiding the capture and punishment that befell so many of the violent men he rode with.

Eventually he had a chance meeting with Fairweather in Kansas City in which Fairweather had laid out a plan for raising the Confederate army again and taking revenge on the North.

While Fairweather spoke of a new America under a Confederate government, White was busily imagining the potential for stealing on a grand scale. He cheerfully volunteered his services as a captain on the spot, assuring Fairweather that the plan was the greatest he had ever heard and that he, Fairweather, would be the first president of the Confederate States of America.

'The men are getting restless, General.'

'Are they?'

'They want to know when we will begin our first major assault on the North.'

'They will know, Captain White, when I choose to tell them.'

White slumped into a chair without invitation. Fairweather sighed but chose to let it go.

'We have had successful raids, General. I think the men are ready for battle.'

'I agree.'

White looked surprised. 'So why. . . ?'

'Simple. We wait on the hostiles.'

'The Indians?'

'Yes.'

'Sir, I think we are wrong to trust those savages.'

The General leaned forward. 'I do not trust them.

However, do you truly think I can take on the whole Union army with what I have camped out around this state?'

'The numbers are growing all the time.'

'Captain, we will be old men before we could launch an attack at this rate. With the entire Indian nation attacking on a second front we can beat the North. The savages are close to joining me, very close. Under a Confederate government I have promised they will have their own lands.'

White could not suppress a sneer. 'And will they get them?'

'Probably, while I still need them. After that who knows? The savages are not the problem. What I need is the negro back in chains where he belongs. They are nothing better than animals and should be used as such.'

White could care less about the blacks, as his chances of ever owning a slave were slim, but he nodded sagely at his general's wise words.

'Tell the men, it will be soon. A new chapter in history is about to be written and they will have their part in it.'

With that he picked up his book and went back to his reading. White stood up, performed a clumsy salute and left the tent.

Connie stood with her arms folded, glowering at him. John was trying to ignore the eyes boring into his back as he packed. It was Connie who broke the

42

angry silence.

'You cannot wait to get that back on, can you?' She pointed at the red tunic that lay across the bed. 'I should have burned it.'

John turned to face her. 'Connie, you are making undue fuss. I will be gone for two or three days at the most. I simply identify who is behind this and where they are, pass that information on to General Reynolds and ride back. You will scarcely notice my absence.'

Connie exploded. 'Of course I will "notice your absence". There will be an empty place at supper. An empty space in the bed beside me.'

'Connie, you are being overly dramatic. I am not going off to war.'

'No, but you wish you were.'

John turned sharply at this. 'Pray what do you mean by that?'

'John, you have been restless for weeks. Do you think I have not noticed it?'

'I have been a little preoccupied with my work. That is all. I am learning a new job.'

'You have not been preoccupied with your work. That is the very nature of the problem. You have been thinking of other things.'

'What other things?'

Connie said simply, 'Adventure.'

John laughed. 'Adventure?'

'Yes, and you see the opportunity to have just that.'

'It is simply intelligence gathering. I will gather and I will return.'

'And you promise me you will avoid any danger?'

'Of course.'

Connie turned away from him sadly. 'Yes, of course.'

She walked back into the living room that she had worked so hard on over the last few weeks, to make a home for John to be proud of. She sat down at the table and fought back the tears. John came into the room carrying his saddlebags and wearing his army uniform. He put the bags down on the floor and went to embrace her but she pushed him away.

'No, no, I will not let you kiss me goodbye. I will not allow it. As far as I am concerned it is just another day. I will not have it as anything else.'

With that she went back into the bedroom and slammed the door. John could hear the sobs beginning to start. He instinctively wanted to go to her and hold her, but he knew that was not what she wanted.

A few minutes later he was riding through Arabella in the thin dawn light. He turned several times to see if Connie had come out on to the porch but it remained empty. He turned up his collar against the morning chill and rode on out of town.

# CHAPTER FIVE

As John rode into St Joseph, Missouri, the sun was just beginning to fade in the late afternoon. It had taken him two days and even though he had managed to find some lodging on the way he was tired and sore. He checked in at the one hotel and then settled Pilot in the livery stable.

A hot bath and a shave later he was sitting in the hotel lobby, still wearing his army uniform and attracting looks from other guests. The uniform was showing signs of the long ride and that suited John's purpose well. He needed to look the part of a man in need of work, and that work was soldiering.

He was trying to identify the agent he had been asked to meet. There were several men obviously staying on their own but they all seemed like businessmen – still, it was hard to tell.

He lit a cigar and picked up a copy of the town newspaper, full of plans for further extension to the

railroad. He was beginning to feel a slight content-
ment coming over him when he heard a discreet
cough nearby.

He lowered his paper to find himself looking into
the face of a young woman probably no older than
himself. She was smartly dressed and her red hair
was neatly pinned back. Her face was beautiful, soft,
with full lips and a firm jaw. She smiled at him.

John was flustered and a little annoyed for a
moment. 'My apologies, madam, is my cigar smoke
troubling you?'

'Not in the least, Captain Carshalton, I enjoy the
smell of a good cigar.'

He began, 'How do you know . . .' And then it
suddenly became painfully obvious how she knew
his name. 'Ah.'

Her smile broadened and he was beginning to
think her one of the most attractive women he had
ever met.

'Quite so, it is I you have arranged to meet.'

He rose to his feet, took her hand and bowed.
'Captain John Carshalton, your servant, madam.'

'It is Miss Charlotte Allen. Pleased to meet you,
Captain. You were expecting a man I'll wager.'

'I do confess, yes.'

She lowered her voice a little. 'I lost three brothers
fighting against people who believe that they can treat
human beings like property. I serve the North in whatever way I can. Anyway,' her voice lightened a little,
'may I thank you for making yourself easy to spot.'

'I am supposed to look like a deserter from the British Army. This is what a deserter from the British army looks like.'

She pointed at the newspaper he had been reading. 'It was more the fact that you can read that alerted me.'

He looked at her to see if she was teasing him. The deep brown eyes were full of merriment.

He relaxed. 'So what do we know so far?'

'Very little beyond what Colonel Reynolds has already told you. Although I do have an idea where one of the camps may be. I went for a ride in the country the day before yesterday. I took a picnic hamper and a story about visiting a sick relative. I spent most of the day following any small trails that I could. Finally, about thirty miles south of here, a young man wearing at least part of a rebel uniform stepped out of the trees, pointed a gun at me and told me it was private land. I tried to question him further but he simply stood there pointing his rifle and threatening to shoot. I rode back to the nearest town, a place called Miller's Crossing. Small, but with an extraordinary amount of men in Confederate uniform. I feigned being lost, but a woman on her own arouses suspicion so I cut out of there.'

John had been listening intently. 'You said "one of the camps".'

'Rumour, and it is only that, is that there is more than one camp. That could be the way they are managing to keep hidden, albeit in an area full of

Confederate sympathizers.'

'But we still do not know who is behind all this.'

'We might. I was stopped in Miller's Crossing reviving myself with coffee after the ordeal of being lost, near fainting as we women are wont to do.' At that point she smiled and laughed, and John could well imagine her putting on quite a show.

'Several times I heard the name General Fairweather mentioned.'

John shrugged, 'Means nothing to me.'

'Nor me', she said regretfully. 'Nor yet the US Army, but still it is a start.'

'So what is expected of me?'

'Very well, here is the plan. Tomorrow you will ride to Miller's Crossing. You will pose as a British deserter. You will say that you have heard that an army is being raised and is looking for recruits. They may simply play dumb, in which case that is probably as far as you can take it. On the other hand they might direct you to the camp, in which case get as much information as you can whilst you are there, report back here and your work is finished.'

John and Charlotte dined together later that evening. She was fine company with a loud laugh that at times unsettled other diners. She talked about her family. Her mother had died when Charlotte was young and she had looked after her father and her three brothers. A great sadness came over her as she talked about her brothers dying in the war and about how her heartbroken father had died within months of the war ending. Just another casualty of war, was her bitter comment before they turned to lighter things.

The next morning he rose early to ride to Miller's Crossing.

It was a small town tucked away near the bank of the Missouri river. In many ways it reminded John of Arabella before Mr Declan Finn had decided to adopt it as his own. He was still not sure how he felt about Declan. The man seemed determined to exercise control over people, and John and Connie in particular. But he had to admit that Arabella had a greater spring in its step than it had before. He just hoped that it would not corrupt people who had been warm and welcoming to a stranger like himself who had been protective of people like Connie.

The main street was busier than he might have expected with a town this size, and he saw what Charlotte meant when she spoke of a surprising number of grey uniforms.

His own red coat was attracting some stares from the local people but he ignored them and tethered his horse in front of the saloon.

Inside all was quiet as he walked in through the swing doors. A piano stood in one corner but with nobody to play it. A few men were drinking at the bar and a game of poker was being played at a small table. Again several of the drinkers glanced in his direction.

He ordered a beer and placed himself at the far end of the bar from the other drinkers. The barman who had served him went back to polishing a large stack of glasses. He looked over at John and decided to make conversation.

'British fella then.'

It was a statement, not a question.

'That is correct.'

'So what brings an English fella to Miller's Crossing?'

John smiled warmly, 'Well, to tell you the truth I did hear that there might be some work to be had.'

'And what kind of work might that be?'

'The sort an ex-soldier might be able to do.'

The small amount of conversation at the end of the bar stilled, and all eyes turned towards him.

The barman stopped cleaning glasses and looked nervously at the other end of the bar. 'Well, mister, I really wouldn't know about anything like that.'

'Who would?'

'Like I say, mister . . .'

'OK Charlie.' A short stocky man wearing the uniform of a sergeant major had detached himself from the drinkers at the bar and approached John.

'My name is Breeze.'

John immediately offered his hand, which was returned, but he noticed that the other man's eyes remained cold and the handshake was brief and less than cordial.

'Captain John Carshalton, late of Her Imperial

Majesty's Army in Canada.'

'How late?'

'I served up until a few months ago.'

'And you're gone for good?'

'Well, I don't think I'll be going back.'

'Is that a fact?'

'No, it is a prediction, but I am sticking to it.'

Breeze seemed to consider John for a moment and then made a decision. 'I think you've been told wrong, Captain. There ain't no soldiering to be done around here.'

John smiled at Breeze again. 'You surprise me when I seem to be surrounded by men in uniform.'

Breeze smiled back coldly. 'Folks around here hankered to the rebel cause. They still wear their uniforms with pride.'

John considered this for a moment. 'That is very understandable and very laudable, I think. Well look, I enjoy the company of soldiers. Why don't you let me buy you a drink and we can talk about our armies?'

'Well I sure would love to do that, Captain, but I have somewhere I have to be. My advice to you is to get back on your horse and ride out the way you came. No good will come of staying around here.'

'If I did not know better, I would assume that you had just threatened me.'

'No, just advice, good advice, but advice for all that.'

Several other men had now moved behind

Breeze and play had stopped in the poker game so that now everybody was watching to see what would happen next.

John took a long pull at his beer. 'All right if I finish my beer?'

'Sure, just don't take too long about it.'

That then, would appear to be that. He had not managed to surmount even the first hurdle. Something about his manner had bothered Breeze, something that he did not like or did not trust. John finished his beer in silence and then left the saloon.

He glanced back over his shoulder, expecting to see triumphant grins on the faces of the men at the bar, but instead he saw only worried expressions following him out.

He mounted Pilot and cantered slowly out of town. Once out of sight of the main street he pulled the horse off the trail and rode up through a large clump of trees until he found a smaller trail winding upwards through the hills.

He followed this for a couple of miles until what he expected to happen happened. A young man in a Confederate uniform several sizes too big for him stepped out from behind a tree and levelled his rifle at John.

'Hold it right there, mister.'

John reined the horse to a halt. He smiled down at the young soldier. 'Good day to you.'

'You are on private property, mister. Just turn your horse about and head back down that trail.'

It was time to gamble.

'I am here to see General Fairweather.' He paused. 'Sergeant Major Breeze sent me.'

The boy looked uncertain. John decided to press his advantage. 'I am Captain John Carshalton, ex-British Army. I have come to fight for the General.' He had no idea if any of that made sense but he had cast his dice and now he just waited.

The boy scratched his smooth chin as if in search of any sign of stubble. At length he lowered the rifle.

'Well, I guess that's all right then.' He stood looking uncertain for a moment and then surprised John by saluting. John returned the salute smartly and then rode on without a word and without looking back, although he could feel the worried gaze of the younger soldier on his back.

After about a mile John rode out of the trees and was immediately in an area of intense activity. Trees were being felled and moved back up the track to where they were being cut and shaped, probably for use in building.

Many of those working on the timber stopped and watched him ride by. Most men were stripped down to their undershirts but all wore Confederate army breeches.

John turned a bend in the trail and then he was approaching a wooden stockade. There were soldiers on the walls and two guarding the open gates. One of these stepped forward with his hand up as John approached. John reined to a halt but before the sentry could speak he leaned forward.

'Captain Carshalton. I have business with General Fairweather.'

'What business?'

John glared at the sentry. 'Are you General Fairweather?'

The soldier looked confused. 'No.'

'Then my business is not with you. I have just left Sergeant Major Breeze.' That much of course was true. John continued, 'So move aside and let me pass, and by the way it is usual to address a commissioned officer as sir, whatever army he is with.'

The soldier looked confused and unhappy.

'I'm sorry, sir, but . . .'

'Let him in, soldier.' The voice came from behind the sentry, who meekly moved aside to let John pass. John found himself moving towards a man in a captain's uniform standing in the centre of what was obviously serving as a parade ground. Several tents surrounded the area and John could see that timber buildings were being constructed. Clearly this was to become a fully functioning fort.

The soldier who had let him pass followed him in.

'Captain White, sir, he says he has just come from the Sergeant Major.'

'The hell you say,' White murmured affably and waved the soldier away.

John dismounted and stood in front of White.

White scowled at John. 'Did I tell you to get down?'

'No, but neither did you tell me not to. In the absence of clear instruction, I decided to seize the initiative.'

White looked confused, but that quickly turned to annoyance.

'So you have just come from Breeze, have you?'

'Yes.'

'Well, if you know anything about soldiering you will know that I outrank Breeze. So I am telling you to turn around and head on back down this trail before I decide to have you arrested.'

'All right, Captain White. I will see this man.'

John looked over White's shoulder at General Fairweather, who had just emerged from one of the tents.

John immediately stood to attention and saluted. White, caught out clumsily, tried to follow suit. Fairweather saw how John had seized the initiative and smiled.

'Stand easy, gentlemen. Captain White, I think it is safe for you to leave us alone.'

'But General, he may be armed.

'Are you armed, Captain Carshalton?'

'I have a revolver in my saddle-bags and the rifle and sword you see on my horse. That is it, General.'

Fairweather smiled at White. 'There you see, Captain, nothing to worry about.'

White scowled at John and turned on his heel and left.

'Take a seat, Captain.' He indicated a small table

with a couple of chairs that stood just outside the entrance to the tent. John was impressed by how well Fairweather moved for a man with one leg. John suspected that his slight build helped. He was a painfully thin man, which made his face gaunter and aged him.

'Thank you, General, that is very kind.'

An elderly soldier appeared from behind John.

'Coffee please, Jackson.'

'Very good, General,' and he was gone.

'I trust you will take refreshment with me, Captain?'

'Honoured, sir, thank you.'

'Now, you say Sergeant Major Breeze sent you?'

'With respect, General, no. I said I had just come from him. That is not quite the same thing.'

Fairweather threw his head back and emitted a braying laugh. 'Ha, you have sand, Captain, by God sir you do.' He paused to let his hilarity subside. 'So, you have gone to all this trouble to see me. What is it you want?'

'To enlist, General.'

'Enlist? Well, well, the British army not paying you sufficiently?'

'They are not paying me at all, General. I no longer hold a commission in the British Army.'

Fairweather did not seem particularly surprised to hear this. 'And what is the reason for that?'

John paused for what he felt was a suitable amount of time to suggest that he was struggling to think what to say next.

'Well, it is this way, sir. I fought a duel knowing that it was against regulations but it was nonetheless a matter of honour. I am sure you will understand, General.'

Indeed he did; matters of honour were something Fairweather could understand. He nodded sympathetically. 'A matter of honour, of course, you had no choice.'

'Thank you, General. As you say, I had no choice and unfortunately the other fellow was killed. There was going to be the most dreadful fuss and you see the matter involved the honour of a young lady from good family and well, need I say more?'

Fairweather felt that John probably could have said more, but he did not want to own to it. 'Ah indeed, of course, in those circumstances.'

'I quit the scene at once and was duly posted as a deserter. And so here I am.'

Fairweather sat back in his chair and steepled his fingers, fondly imagining that this made him look thoughtful and wise.

'I do not believe, Captain, that you are telling me the whole truth.'

John froze. At what point had he slipped up? It had all sounded reasonably plausible as he was telling it.

'Your name is familiar. Was there not the matter of your being involved in a shoot-out in some small town in Kansas?'

John felt relief and surprise in equal measure.

'You have heard about that, General?'

'I read the newspapers, Captain. The Eastern papers were full of it. Very heroic stuff by the sound of it.'

'As always, General, the newspapers tend to exaggerate.'

'There was talk of you becoming town sheriff, I think.'

'I did consider it, sir, but when all is said and done, I am a soldier. So when I heard rumours that there was something rather exciting happening, well it was the call I needed.'

'Hmm, exciting, you thought?'

'Oh very much, General. Of course I am not privy to your plans but looking around me I suspect that you feel, as many of us do, that the war between the states ended with the wrong result.'

Fairweather beamed and slapped the table. 'There, have I not always said it. The British understand. They appreciate that power and authority belong with the wealthy and the influential. The North is run by fools. All this bleeding-heart nonsense over the negro, who is no better than an animal. Allowing in every cut-throat murderer that every other nation on earth wants rid of. It has to be put right. This land needs people like me to protect it from itself. I will build a wall around this country, Carshalton. We are going to change history.'

John wore what he hoped was an enthusiastic

smile. 'I want to be part of that, General.'

'Do you, do you, by God? Then you shall be. I need an officer like you. Oh, do not get me wrong, White is a stout fellow right enough, but rough around the edges. Hard to understand how he got his commission but, time of war I suppose. Anyway I need an officer who is well educated and well bred. A man trained to be a soldier. See here, Carshalton, let me explain what is happening here.'

The coffee arrived and for the next two hours Fairweather enthusiastically explained to John his plan for taking back America for what he called 'true Americans'. He talked of the other small camps he had set up all over Missouri and the Carolinas. He talked of the begged, borrowed and stolen military hardware. He talked of the financial support from fellow 'visionaries', and of course the Ku Klux Klan. And he talked of the one thing that sent a chill down John's spine; the alliance he was forming with the Indian nations.

'Imagine it, Carshalton, all over America, Indian tribes rising, fighting the kind of guerilla war they are good at. We could run the US Army ragged. We could cut their supply lines. Destroy their economy. We could paralyse this present government into sub-mission.

'Once the centre of the new Confederate govern-ment is established in Richmond we will destroy the savages. We will have no more use for them and they have no place in a civilized country. Well,

59

Carshalton, what do you think?'

John would dearly have loved to tell Fairweather what he thought and then shot him, but surrounded as he was by the new army of Northern Virginia this did not seem like a good plan. He struggled for words.

'General, it is like nothing I have ever heard. It is ... extraordinary. By which I mean exceptional.'

Fairweather listened eagerly. 'Exceptional, you think so?'

'I can honestly say, General, that this plan is without equal. It is the product of a mind the like of which you only encounter occasionally.'

'You mean that?'

'Most sincerely, sir.'


'He is mad, of course. I don't just mean powercrazed mad, I mean full-blown howling at the moon mad. I mean, queue up and pay a penny to see him in Bedlam kind of mad.'

'So it would seem,' Charlotte agreed, as she and John sat sipping brandy in front of the fire at the hotel that evening.

'Mind,' John continued, 'he would not be the first madman to cause a war on a massive scale and sadly he will in all probability not be the last.'

'I have written your report and an army rider has already taken it off to Colonel Reynolds.'

'So that is that?'

'Indeed it is. You have done well, red soldier, but

your work here is done. You are free to return home.'

He could not help but feel a little tinge of disappointment. He did not feel that he had done so terribly much other than gain access to a madman who could not wait to tell every part of his plan.

He looked across at Charlotte and noticed how the firelight reflected off her hair. She was, he thought, truly a very attractive woman.

'You find me attractive, red soldier?'

John jumped guiltily. Had he said that out loud?

She laughed lightly at his guilty expression. 'I can tell by the way you look at me.'

'I'm sorry,' he stammered. 'I meant no disrespect. I . . . I only . . .'

She shushed him gently. 'Don't apologize to a woman for finding her attractive.' She rested her hand on top of his. 'You are a very handsome man. I am flattered.'

He looked awkwardly at her small hand on top of his. He cleared his throat, 'Charlotte, I am a married man.'

She laughed loudly at this. 'Good Heavens, did you think I was going to throw myself on top of you?'

'No, no, of course not. I simply meant . . . that is I didn't mean to imply . . .'

She laughed again and held up her hand. 'I am teasing you, red soldier. I know you have a very pretty wife to go back to. I would like to say that she is a lucky woman.'

John looked surprised. 'But you find you cannot?'

'No, and I will tell you why.' For a moment she looked sad. 'Because you will break her heart.'

'I have no such intention.'

'Of course you do not, but you will, notwith-standing.'

'I do not understand.'

'No, red soldier, you do not. You see, in my expe-rience there are two kinds of killer in the world. There is the stone-cold killer born to kill, God never had any other plan for him, it is what he must do. And then there are killers like you.'

'I do not consider myself a killer.'

'And yet you have killed, and you will again. Except for you it is all wrapped up in duty and honour. You cannot avoid it. You cannot turn away from what you believe to be a just cause, a just reason to fight. Tell me, when you left home was your wife crying?'

'Yes.'

'And yet you left.'

'I had made a commitment to Colonel Reynolds.'

His voice trailed off. Charlotte smiled sadly. 'Your wife will try to change you. She will not succeed and because she loves you she will learn to bear it. I know, I watched three brothers who I loved more than anything in the world march off to war and no amount of entreaty could stop them. We are what God made us, red soldier.'

She caught the eye of a passing waiter, 'More brandy I think.'

*

John slept well and in the morning rose early to pack his bags and be on his way. He checked out and was gathering his things to take over to the livery stable when Colonel Reynolds stepped into the lobby.

'Ah, Captain Carshalton, I am relieved that I have caught you.' He shook John's hand. 'Excellent report, Captain. Splendid work. However, if we could just have a word.'

John looked puzzled. 'Of course. Concerning what?'

'Well, I am afraid to ask but there is just one more thing I would like you do.'

# CHAPTER SIX

They sat in the lobby of the hotel, a pot of coffee largely untouched on the table between them. Charlotte sat near to John and for once she was not smiling. Her lips were pressed tight together and her fingers were drumming soundlessly on the padded arm of the chair.

Reynolds was speaking. 'I agree completely that from everything you have said Fairweather is quite insane. That does not make him any less dangerous. However, we now have enough information to attack his camps and bring him down. The problem, of course, is the hostile Indians. We are only a few years out of the most savage war in our history – in anybody's history – and since then we have had conflict with the Indians. The last thing we need now is another Indian war. For all we know he could have hostiles close to him. If we attack we could find ourselves, for instance, facing the entire Sioux nation.'

John shifted uneasily, 'I agree with everything you

64

say, sir, but I fail to see how I can be of any assistance.'

'We need somebody to meet with the Indians. We need to understand how close this alliance is. We need to persuade them that Fairweather is mad and that he will lead them to destruction.'

'Colonel, I have no experience of dealing with Indians either here or in Canada. I have scarcely seen an Indian, let alone conversed with one.'

'That is the point, John. You will be seen as a neutral. Frankly, the Indians do not trust us.'

'I wonder why that would be?' Charlotte murmured.

Reynolds chose to ignore her. 'They will see you as English, not American. You could win their trust.'

'The trust of whom, Colonel? Every tribe in the United States? Who do I go to?'

'You need to find out who Fairweather negotiates with. You have to find them and talk to them.'

Charlotte leaned forward. 'That means going back into that camp. That means risking being found out. John has done what he was asked to do. He has every right to go home to his wife.'

The colonel nodded, 'Yes, he does. I cannot order you, John, but I am asking you to help us avoid a terrible conflict with great loss of life.'

John looked miserably at the ceiling. Charlotte reached over and put her hand on his as she had the night before when she had been teasing him. This time the grip was firm.

'You don't have to do this, John.' There was a pleading look in her eye. She looked deep into his eyes and then sighed and leaned back and shook her head. 'Your mind is already made up. How quickly you prove me right.'

She rose and without a backward glance at either of the men climbed the stairs to her room.

John looked miserably at his saddlebags with his rifle and sword on the floor nearby. All ready to saddle Pilot and head back to the arms of Connie, and beer on the porch with Josh.

He sighed. 'Very well.'

Josh was just lighting his first pipe of the day and leaning back in the swivel chair to read the latest handbills sent down from Abilene when the door burst open and Connie stormed in. Such was the force of her arrival that Josh almost tipped backwards on the chair. He grabbed for the edge of the desk and in doing so swung himself round so that he was facing the wall with his back to Connie.

'Josh, where is he?'

Josh swung the seat back to face Connie, who was leaning over the desk to receive him. He opened his mouth to speak and Connie leaned closer.

'Say "who", Josh, I challenge you, just say "who" and I will knock you clean out of that chair.'

'You mean John.'

'Damn right I mean John.'

Josh tried to wrest back control. 'Now see here

66

Connie, you can't just stomp in here shouting at a fella who ain't done nothing. Who's put a burr under your saddle anyhow?'

'Doc Freeman has.'

'The doc? Why, are you sick?'

'Frequently, mostly in the mornings.'

Josh smiled, 'Well heck, girl, that's probably just eating too many underripe apples. Hell, fruit can play my stomach up something awful . . .'

Connie grabbed hold of Josh's shirtfront. 'I mean I am having a baby, you idiot.'

'Now Connie, there is no good reason to be calling folks names . . . ah . . .'

Connie released his shirtfront. 'Yes, "ah". Get him back, Josh, I need him here now.'

'Well see here, Connie, it's just not that easy.'

'Why isn't it?'

'Well for a start, I don't rightly know where he is.'

Connie had exhausted her anger for a moment and sat down heavily on the chair in front of the desk. Josh looked concerned. Like all men who had never been fathers Josh looked on pregnant women as some kind of bomb about to explode. Then he reasoned, Connie was always like some kind of bomb about to explode.

'Are you all right, Connie? Can I get you a glass of water?'

'No, Josh, I do not want water. I want my husband back.'

'Well like I say, I don't rightly know. . . .'

67

'What do you know?'

Josh sighed, 'I know he was going to Missouri.'

Connie stared at him, 'Missouri? Where in Missouri?'

'St Joe, I think.'

Connie shook her head, 'That must be two days' ride from here.' She mimicked angrily, "I'll only be gone for two days, three at the most". What is he riding, Winged Pegasus?'

She was proud of having jumped for that reference. During her time in Canada she had learned to read and one of the books she had learned from was a book of Greek myths; she had particularly liked the story of the winged horse.

'What's Pegasus?'

'Never mind. What was he going to do when he got to St Joe?'

'He had to meet this agent fella.'

'Agent? What kind of agent?'

'The secret kind I guess. The US Government kind.'

For the first time Connie looked lost. 'Josh, what is going on?'

'Look, Connie, all I know is this. There's been some raids over the border in the last few months. Put people in mind of Bleeding Kansas.'

'Of what?'

'Before the war there was a lot of bad blood between the pro-slavers in Missouri and the anti-slavers in Kansas. Blood was spilled. Folks said it was the real start of the war. And it seems to be happening again.'

'John said it was just some intelligence gathering for the US Army.'

'And so it is. John just had to find out where these raids are coming from, tell the army and that's it.'

'So where is he?'

'Heck, he probably just wants to do a thorough report. You know John.'

Connie laughed bitterly, 'Oh yes, I know John. The minute he put that dammed uniform on he was back fighting for Queen and country. Leading the cavalry charge. Damn it, he couldn't see two wildcats fighting without wanting to get involved. His mother warned me.'

'You met his mother?'

'Yes.'

'What was she like?'

Connie face clouded, 'Nice, really nice.'

She remembered how nervous she had been at meeting John's mother, when she was presented to this tall woman who had clearly been a beauty all her life and who fixed Connie with a searching stare that seemed to bore right into her.

A lesser girl than Connie might have quailed and looked away and at that moment she certainly wanted to. But she knew John was worth fighting for and the Irish in her made her return the stare, forcing her to look upwards and involuntarily jut out her chin. For a moment both women looked into each other's eyes and then the warmest of smiles broke out on Mrs Carshalton's face.

'Oh yes,' she had said approvingly, 'you will do, you will do very well indeed.'

Connie was not sure that she wanted 'to do', but the sincerity of the smile could not be mistaken and neither could the hug that followed. From then on Connie had been welcomed into the family and John's mother treated her as the daughter she had always longed for.

As she remembered this now the tears welled up in her eyes. 'Get him back for me, Josh, please. Go to St Joe, find the agent fella and tell him John has to come back. Tell him I need him more than the US Army does. They're not having his baby.'

'Connie, I can't just drop everything and go. It will leave Arabella without a lawman.'

'Tell Abilene and they will send a deputy down. They have done it before. Damn it, Josh, I will keep law and order if I have to.'

Josh grinned, 'Damned if you wouldn't at that. All right, girl, I'll go and get him back in one piece.'

Connie smiled through her tears, grabbed Josh's hand and pressed it to her cheek.

# CHAPTER SEVEN

John rode back up to Fairweather's camp with somewhat less confidence than on his earlier visit. It was quite one thing to bluff for a couple of hours, altogether a different thing to live and walk amongst men who could discover at any time that he was not what he pretended to be.

He was also thinking of Connie. He had lied to her from the outset by suggesting that his mission was altogether a more local affair. Now he had failed to contact her by telegraph and tell her what was happening. He deeply regretted that now. He knew she would be worried, but what was done was done and he must continue with his mission.

Within a short time of arriving back in the camp his British red tunic was replaced by Confederate grey. The uniform felt uncomfortable in every sense, but it did seem that in a very short time he was being accepted as another soldier.

Sergeant Major Breeze had not been best pleased

at having his name taken in vain to allow John access to Fairweather. However, Breeze was a professional soldier and a pragmatist and decided that officers did bad things, but for all that they were officers and should be treated as such.

Indeed over the first few days Breeze began to take quite a liking to John. He felt it was refreshing to have an officer who was neither mad nor an over-promoted thug.

Over the next few days, John drilled, trained and prepared Fairweather's rag-tag army, all the time bringing himself further and further into the General's trust, to the annoyance of Captain White.

John also used his time to gain more insight into White's motives for being part of all this. It did not take much finding out. It became abundantly clear that White was an outlaw, a renegade like Jesse James and John Wesley Harding, albeit a pale imitation of either. He had a group of around a dozen men, some of whom he had known for years, none of whom had strayed too close to the battles of the Civil War.

It became increasingly obvious that White planned to loot as much as he could once the real fighting started and then disappear.

John did consider telling Fairweather this, but it was something that could misfire and it was also not why he had returned to the camp.

The chance to fulfil his mission finally came one morning when John was alone with Fairweather and the General let slip that he had to ride to meet his Indian contact, a journey which, with his one leg, he did not much favour.

John dived straight in. 'Is this something I could help you with, General? I have extensive experience of liaising with the native Indians in Canada and I would be pleased to go in your place.'

Fairweather looked unsure. 'I appreciate the thought, Captain, but one has to be careful with the savages. Damn touchy the Indians, especially the chiefs. All pumped up with their own self-importance.'

John could see that in that case it would be a meeting of the like-minded but he pressed on. 'I can easily say you are at a critical stage in your preparations, which of course, sir, is not untrue. I would expect to be fully briefed by yourself, of course, as to what I can or cannot mention.'

Fairweather thought a little more. 'Well,' he said at length, 'it is a damnably tempting offer.'

At that John knew he had succeeded, and the following day he rode out fully instructed as to the messages he was to give the Indian contact.

The man he was riding west to meet was a chief called He-Dog, of a small Oglala Lakota band known as the Cankahuhan or Soreback that was closely associated with Red Cloud's Bad Face band of Oglala. He knew that He-Dog was trusted by Red Cloud and many of the other Sioux and Cheyenne tribes. He would have liked to know more about the man himself but he would find that out soon enough.

He was riding deep into Kansas, where He-Dog had travelled for the sole purpose of negotiating with Fairweather on the alliance between the new Confederate army and the Indian nation.

He rode up towards Nebraska and into the hills. That night he slept under the stars for the first time in a long time and enjoyed the feeling of freedom that it gave. He liked the night sounds and fullness of the clear sky. Not for the first time he felt how much he loved this country with all its vastness and surprises, and the feeling of newness and excitement that it generated. Then he thought of Fairweather, who only wanted to restart a dreadful war and men like White who only knew stealing and killing. He drifted off thinking of Connie and the home they could make together in America.

He awoke feeling refreshed but also with the realization that he had slept longer than he planned.

He pushed on quickly but it was late morning when he reached the outskirts of He-Dog's camp. As he rode up the trail leading through large rocks on both sides warriors began to appear above him. They were not painted and they simply stood almost dispassionately watching him ride by. Nobody moved and nobody spoke, but he knew that the news of his arrival was being passed up the line.

Eventually near the top of the hill he entered the camp. He had expected only warriors to be present, but women were hard at work preparing food and children ran about. The children ran excitedly up to him and followed him, laughing and calling words he did not understand until a warrior shouted at them and they scattered.

A man emerged from a tent and John knew at once that it was He-Dog; he carried with him that air of quiet authority that he had heard described of the chiefs of the tribes north of the border.

He dismounted, and at once a warrior stepped forward and took his horse. He felt suddenly exposed in the middle of the camp and unsure what to do next. He decided to take the initiative and stepped towards He-Dog, held out his hand and bowed stiffly.

'Captain John Carshalton at your service, sir.'

He-Dog looked slightly amused but took the offered hand. John was surprised that the grip was not as firm as he might have expected, but suspected that the man was probably not comfortable with that type of greeting.

A young man appeared behind He-Dog. John could see at once that he was white even though his skin was darkened by constant living in the open.

'My birth name is Harry Bristow and my Indian name is Boy Who Digs Yellow Stones. My pa was a miner, he took me with him. When I was ten the Indians killed Pa and took me. These are my people now. I will tell He-Dog your words exactly as you tell me. I will do the same with his words to you.'

John nodded that he understood.

He was preparing to sit cross-legged on the ground when a warrior appeared carrying a small oak table of the kind that had probably once held a sewing machine. John did not like to think where that might have come from. Two chairs were also produced and He-Dog and John sat across from each other. He-Dog said a few words which Bristow translated. 'He-Dog asks if you would take tea. He-Dog likes tea.'

'I am British. I like tea.'

Conversation was beginning to flow between He-Dog and John, and Bristow rapidly translated.

'I expected General Fairweather.'

'The General sends his deepest regrets. He is at a crucial time in his planning for his war on the US Government.'

'Why is an Englishman wearing that uniform?'

'I have left the British Army. I have joined General Fairweather.'

They passed pleasantries for a few minutes until the tea arrived. It came in a battered silver teapot with two chipped cups. John was struck by the absurdity of the scene. All it took, he reflected, was a plate of dainty sandwiches and they could have been sitting on an English lawn taking tea with the parson.

'So,' He-Dog said at length, 'what news do you have for me?'

John took a deep breath. He stopped talking

towards Bristow as he had been and now leaned forward so that he was speaking directly to He-Dog.

'He-Dog, what I am about to say could cost me my life if it is told to General Fairweather.'

There was a slight hesitation from Bristow. John looked sharply at him and nodded for him to continue. As the words were translated he saw the other man stiffen and the cold flinty eyes seemed to stare into him.

'I am what I said I am. I am or was a captain in the army of Her Imperial Majesty Queen Victoria. I am now the sheriff for a small town near Abilene. I was asked by the United States Army to find out what General Fairweather was planning.'

He-Dog's lip curled. 'I have little respect for men who pretend to be what they are not.'

'The United States Government is desperate to avoid a war with Indian nations which can only end in misery and bloodshed. Red Cloud has made a peace. There is a treaty in place. It must be given time to work.'

He-Dog sneered, 'Treaties last until the white man wants something. To build a railroad, to dig for yellow stones, to drive their cattle through our sacred lands. If we ride with Fairweather we can defeat the US soldiers. Fairweather has promised us our own lands, our own part of this country. It will be in the North West. If will belong to all the tribes. It will be as it was before the white man came.'

'I know you have been lied to, He-Dog, but

77

Fairweather is just another liar. General Fairweather has told you he has a great army. He does not. He has hundreds, not thousands, of soldiers as he claims. He relies on you and the great chiefs for his army. It is your warriors who will die in their thousands to give power to Fairweather.

'Fairweather is mad. I have listened to his schemes. They are those of a man who has lost his wits. But I will tell you this, He-Dog, he has explained to me that when you have helped him to become the great president commanding all the army he plans to wipe you and all your people out of existence.'

Bristow's voice trailed off and there was silence.

He-Dog stared at John for what seemed an age. At length he spoke again. 'Why should I believe you any more than I can believe any white man?'

'Simply this, He-dog. I am going to leave here and go back to Fairweather's camp. I am going to tell him that I have delivered the messages that he asked me to and nothing more. All you have to do is send a trusted brave to tell Fairweather the truth of what has been said here and I will be killed. I am putting my life in your hands.'

The silence returned when Bristow had finished. After a time He-Dog spoke again. 'You will spend tonight in one of my lodges. You will not be harmed. In the morning I will give you my thoughts. If you leave in the night I will know that you spoke falsely.'

'I will be here when the sun rises, He-Dog, that I promise.'

And he was. He sat on the hill looking down towards the Great Plains, trying to figure his next move. If He-Dog completely rejected what John had told him then John had little choice but to cut and run. He would have failed completely, and John was not a man who often took failure as an option.

Harry Bristow appeared beside him. 'He-Dog will see you now.'

John rose and followed him back to He-Dog's lodge. No table was set up this time and there was no sign of tea. This was obviously not going to be a long discussion.

He-Dog stepped out of the teepee as John approached. He started to speak as soon as John was close and Bristow had to rush ahead to hear what the man was saying.

'I thought through the night about your words, Captain. I do not know if I can trust you but you look me straight in the eye when you speak with me, and that makes He-Dog feel easier in his mind. I will take your words to Red Cloud and I will take the counsel of the other chiefs. You can ride away now in peace, Captain. No word of our talk yesterday will leave this camp.'

John tried not to look too relieved. 'He-Dog has been both wise and just. My words were intended to avoid bloodshed. I hope that your great chiefs will believe me.'

He-Dog simply nodded curtly and stepped back into his teepee. Their meeting was over.

John saddled Pilot and rode off down the trail. This time there were no warriors to watch him. He was no longer to be feared. As he rode out towards the Great Plains he knew he must now return to Fairweather. He had sown the seeds of doubt in He-Dog, and now he must try to do the same to the General.

Josh left Arabella in the dawn light. He knew that he was trying to find a man in the vastness of Kansas and Missouri and he had little idea how to start. He pulled his collar up against the chill of the early morning air and pointed his horse towards St Joseph.

When John rode back into Fairweather's camp the next day it seemed busier than ever. There appeared to be more soldiers camping inside the fort. Brought up, he assumed, from one of the other camps. White, as always, scowled at him as he went past and went back to sharing a jug with the dozen or so NCOs that made up his social circle.

Breeze had seen him arrive and was waiting outside his tent to take his horse. He saluted smartly, which John returned before climbing wearily down from Pilot.

'General's compliments, sir, and asked to see you as soon as you got in.'

'Thanks, Sergeant Major.'

John crossed the parade ground to Fairweather's

tent. He stopped outside. 'Captain Carshalton reporting as requested.'

Fairweather's voice sounded slightly shrill and agitated. 'Yes, yes, Captain, come along.'

John stepped inside the tent. Fairweather was at his writing table studying a map by the light of a lamp. 'Come in, Captain, take a seat.' He tore himself away from the map. 'Now, how did it go with He-Dog?'

'Not sure, General.'

' "Not sure", damn it, sir, what do you mean "not sure"?'

'He seemed a little lukewarm to the message I was giving him.'

'You told it to him exactly as I ordered? You explained that I now have the first wagonload of repeating rifles which Red Cloud has been so anxious to get his hands on?'

'Of course sir, word for word,' John felt he was becoming a more proficient liar with each passing day. 'I wondered if he was getting cold feet.'

' "Cold feet"? Damn it, man, he is an Indian chief, not some frightened virgin on her wedding night.'

'Yes, sir.'

Fairweather sat back and steepled his fingers in what was by now a familiar pose. They both sat in silence for some minutes. John decided that Fairweather had detected the lie and retribution would follow. Suddenly the General sighed and sat forward.

'Damn it, I should have seen this. Felt at our last meeting that something was wrong. Wretched savages – no spine, that's the trouble, no spine. Great when they are attacking women and children in wagon trains, no damn stomach for a battle.'

John sat in stunned silence. He had not predicted this. It was a measure of how much Fairweather trusted him.

Fairweather banged his fist on the table. 'Well, he's going to damn well fight whether he likes it or not. This situation needs remedying. Carshalton, go and freshen up and get yourself something to eat. I want you and White back here in an hour. We are going to light a fire under He-Dog.'

When Josh rode into St Joseph it was almost dusk. It had been a long ride and he, like John, had slept out in the open for the first time in a long time, but unlike John he found nothing uplifting or romantic in it. His bones ached from sleeping on the hard ground and the old bayonet wound from the war throbbed angrily.

He dismounted and hitched his horse outside the hotel. He entered and trudged over to the desk. He checked in, made arrangements for his horse to be taken to the livery stable and then asked the clerk if he knew John.

'Captain Carshalton checked out almost a week ago, Mr Ramsey.'

'Did he say where he was headed?'

'No sir, I am afraid not.'

Josh sighed. To have missed him by that much was frustrating, but what on earth was he doing to be gone that long? This sounded a lot more than intelligence gathering. He had a sinking feeling that Connie was right to have been worried.

As he made to climb the stairs he became aware of an attractive red-haired woman watching. He shrugged it off as mere fancy and climbed the stairs to a hot bath.


John presented himself back at Fairweather's tent in one hour as requested and arrived at the same time as White, whose natural scowl deepened as he saw John.

'Know what this is about, Carshalton?'

'Not really. The General was not happy with the report I gave him on my meeting with He-Dog.'

White sneered, 'Shouldn't have sent a boy to do a man's job then.'

John was about to retort when Fairweather shouted from inside the tent. 'Will you two get in here, instead of standing gossiping like old women.'

They both entered the tent. John saluted smartly, White did the usual sullen sweep of his hand in the general direction of his head.

'Sit down you two, and listen.'

Both the captains pulled up chairs and sat opposite Fairweather.

'Captain Carshalton has confirmed what I was beginning to suspect. He-Dog is starting to have second thoughts.'

White raised an eyebrow in surprise but said nothing.

'My fault for trusting the damned heathens. Well, I think it is soon put right. What they need is a nudge in the right direction.'

He thumped his finger down on the map opened on the table in front of him. 'See here,' he was pointing to a spot over the border in Iowa by the Missouri river. 'Small village, a few warriors, mostly weavers and canoe builders. They live a peaceful life and let the world go by. Well the world is about to pay them a visit, gentlemen. Or to be more precise, the US Cavalry is about to pay them a visit.'

Both John and White looked baffled.

Fairweather was enjoying the bewilderment of his officers. 'I have enough stolen US army uniforms to dress a company of our cavalry to the point where survivors, and we will make sure there are survivors, just not many of them, will clearly identify the United States Cavalry as the perpetrators of this ghastly deed. The uniforms will not be complete but they will serve. See if He-Dog can convince the other chiefs not to follow us then. Well, gentlemen, what do you think?'

Josh came down to the lobby of the hotel with supper on his mind, but first he headed to the bar flor a cold beer and to sit and think about his next move. As sometimes happens, his next move was thought out for him.

As he sat sipping his beer and wondering how he was going to go back home and tell Connie he had lost her husband, he became aware that the red-haired woman he had noticed earlier was standing over him.

She smiled as he looked up and he instinctively rose and tipped his hat. 'Can I help you, ma'am?'

'Well, you can start by asking me to sit down.'

Josh found himself thinking that if she was a whore than she was possibly the classiest whore he had ever met.

'Of course, ma'am. Can I get you some refreshment?' He found he was talking the way he did to the clergyman's wife.

'No thank you, not at the moment.' She sat down opposite him and smoothed out her skirts.

'I will come straight to the point, sir. I believe I heard you earlier enquiring after John Carshalton.'

Josh frowned. 'Why, yes I did. Do you happen to know John?'

'Yes, I do, but before we go on I have to be sure who I am speaking with. Would you by any chance be Josh?'

Josh found himself answering guardedly, 'Yes I would.'

She smiled again and relaxed somewhat. 'And you do match the description he gave.'

'Which was?'

'Perhaps better I do not go into that.'

Josh allowed himself a smile. 'And may I ask who you are, ma'am?'

'My name is Charlotte Allen.'

'And how did you come to meet John?' Damn fool question looking at you, he thought, but then this is John we are talking about and not a man about to fall for the first pretty face he sees.

'I met John quite deliberately. I am the US Government Agent John was sent here to work with.'

Josh sat for a moment letting this sink in. 'But you are a woman . . . a lady.'

'Yes, hopefully I can be both.'

'But I was expecting a man.'

'I am so sorry to have disappointed you.'

Josh grinned. 'Well you sure haven't done that, Charlotte, it's just that I am an old timer and I cannot get used to the things women get up to now.'

Charlotte laughed loudly at this, causing several heads to turn.

'Anyways,' he continued, 'do you know where John is?'

Her smile faded. 'I knew where he was.' She went on to tell Josh all that had happened. Josh listened with increasing alarm.

'He went on his own to meet Indians?'

'Not at my request, I assure you, quite the opposite, but Colonel Reynolds can be a very persuasive man.'

Josh felt that he would need to be to stop Josh

from beating the man black and blue, but he kept that to himself.

'I expected that once he had met with the Indian contact he would return here. I must assume that he has gone back to the army camp, but I cannot think why he would.'

Or his scalp is hanging on an Indian lance, he thought. He knew that Charlotte was thinking the same thing.

'OK,' he said abruptly, 'what happens now? And I will tell you, Charlotte, I ain't good at waiting.'

'Very well. What I suggest is this. John said you were a soldier in the army, yes?'

'Fought for the Union.'

'Yes, well, best keep that to yourself. Tomorrow you could ride up to the army camp and offer to enlist. Whether they take you or not it should give you time to look around and see if John is there.'

Josh stroked his chin, 'Well I can't come up with anything better, so I'll do it.'

Her warm smile had returned. 'But first I buy you supper.'

'I don't think that's the way it is done, ma'am.'

'Oh, don't worry. I will not be paying for it, the US Government will. As somebody who has been a soldier and a lawman I would suggest the government owes you.'

They rose to go through to the dining room. He could see that Charlotte was worried behind the warm smile. 'Don't fret over John too much,' he said reassuringly, 'that Englishman has got nine lives.'

She smiled gratefully at him. 'Yes, but how many has he already used up?'

Josh sighed. 'That, Charlotte, is a very good question.'

John's head was in a whirl. Whatever he had expected on returning to the camp this was not it.

To John's intense relief Fairweather had decided that the Englishman did not have sufficient cavalry experience to lead the attack on the village. It therefore fell to White to lead, having as he did, Fairweather had previously been assured, substantial experience as a cavalry captain.

John almost smiled at the look of horror that passed over White's face. He quickly hid it, but there could be no doubt that White had rather exaggerated his prowess in this particular area.

Beyond that John did not feel much like smiling. Far from stopping bloodshed he had now condemned an entire Indian village. He scarcely listened as Fairweather excitedly prattled on about the best route into the village to attack, how to ensure that their flank was not turned, to use the element of surprise. He talked as though he was taking on the might of Napoleon's army instead of a village full of non-hostile natives.

'Drive through and drive them into the river,' he advised White, 'but make sure you leave a couple alive who will testify to the fact that these were US

Army. God knows they have done it before, so it will not take much believing.'

That, John thought was certainly true. Only recently Lieutenant Colonel George Armstrong Custer's 7th cavalry in what was, without any apparent irony, named The Battle of Washita River, attacked a village of sleeping Cheyenne that included Chief Black Kettle, leaving, according to Custer, some 140 warriors plus some women and children killed, and 53 women and children taken hostage. The Indians, John reflected, had no cause to trust any white man, and he was about to add to this appalling catalogue of atrocities committed by both sides.

As Fairweather talked and John thought, he eventually knew what he had to do. When the General finally dismissed White and himself he hung back as White left.

'Something I can do for you, Captain?'

'Er yes, General, I wonder if I could have your permission to visit some of the other camps.'

'May I ask why?'

'Yes, sir. I am very conscious that once the hostilities commence you will want soldiers who have previously not trained or lived together to unite as a cohesive unit. To that end I would like them to at least become accustomed to one of the officers who will be leading them. As I am sure you know from your own invaluable experience of leadership, the trust of the men is paramount.'

Indeed it is, Fairweather thought ruefully, but he beamed at John with the madness of imagined battles burning in his eyes. 'But, of course, Captain, what a splendid thought. Capital, capital, go ahead by all means.'

'Thank you, General, I will leave first thing in the morning so as to minimize my time away from camp.'

He slept little that night and rose with the dawn. He left the camp riding slowly south until he was out of sight of the sentries and then took a trail to his right and once he was clear of the trees lit out west towards the Great Plains.

# CHAPTER EIGHT

Following the directions given by Charlotte, Josh began to push his horse gently up the trail towards the Confederate army camp. His hope was that he would find John there and at least get some idea what was going on. He was so lost in thought he almost did not see the young sentry stepping out in front of him.

'Hold it right there, mister.'

He reined in the horse and waited as the soldier advanced on him.

'This is private land, mister. You need to turn that horse right around and ride back down that trail.'

Josh forced a smile when all he really wanted to do was take the rifle off the boy and beat his behind with it. 'Now see here, son, that's no way to treat a new recruit.'

The boy sneered. 'You ain't no recruit, Pops, and we got all the cooks and bottle washers we need. Anyways, what do you know about it?'

'Some.' An idea occurred to Josh. 'I got talking to this English fella, Captain somebody . . .'

For the first time the boy looked uncertain, 'Captain Carshalton?'

'That was the fella. Well, he said he couldn't make no promises but he was looking to recruit old soldiers like me. All I want is a quick word with him.'

The boy was caught in two minds. 'Well, I guess.'

'Thanks, son, much obliged.' Josh gave the boy no more time to consider, just spurred the horse past him and onwards up the trail.

When he arrived at the fort, he was, as he expected, stopped again. He repeated his story. This time he had a less credulous audience.

The sergeant he was addressing looked unimpressed. 'That don't sound like the Captain to me. He's not one to be loose at the mouth. Anyways, the Captain rode out this morning and he ain't expected back for a few days.'

Josh's heart sank. 'Did he happen to say where he was going?'

The sergeant grinned. 'Why yes, he did happen to say, but he didn't happen to say that I should tell his business to every old timer who comes up here asking questions. Now git, old man, before I lose patience.'

There was nothing left to do but turn his horse around and ride back down the trail. He had no idea where John was and what he was up to, but one thing that Josh knew in his heart was that whichever way John was riding it would not be away from danger.

John was taking a great risk, even by his standards. He was riding hard into an Indian camp without being expected. He prayed that Bristow would be on hand to interpret, otherwise things could become difficult.

He drove Pilot hard up the trail to the camp. He saw the warriors on the rocks again but this time they looked unsure and a few of them raised bows ready to shoot, but there were shouts from behind them and they hesitated. As he rode into the camp more weapons were snatched up and again metal-tipped arrows were pointing at him.

He-Dog came out of his teepee as John dismounted and to his relief he could see Bristow running from the other side of the camp.

Bristow looked angry. 'Are you crazy? Riding in here like this? Do you want to get yourself killed?'

He-Dog was standing looking coldly at him.

John was unsure whether or not to offer his hand and decided against.

'I have important news for He-Dog.'

He-Dog nodded curtly.

As quickly as he was able John related to He-Dog what had taken place with Fairweather. He described the location of the village by the Missouri river and the fact that the Confederates would be dressed up to look like US Cavalry.

When he had finished there was a long silence. John had learned patience where He-Dog was concerned and stood and waited. Eventually He-Dog began to speak as Bristow interpreted.

'I have been asking questions about you, Captain Carshalton.'

John's heart sank.

'You are a . . .' he paused, 'I think the word is "deserter". That means soldier who runs away. You were brought before your chiefs because you had run away. Is that true, Captain Carshalton?'

John felt desperate and alone. 'It is true but . . .'

'Then why should I trust you? You could be setting a trap. You have been proved to be a man without honour.'

John drew himself up and stared straight into He-Dog's eyes. 'He-Dog, the reason that I ran is that I had fought a duel. It was a fair fight. We both had pistols. We both fired. My ball struck the other and killed him. It had not been my intention. Do my words make sense to you?'

He-Dog nodded curtly.

'It was against the rules of the British Army. My actions threatened to embarrass people I cared about. I took bad advice from a friend. I wanted only to absent myself until things calmed down but then I was followed by the brother of the man I had killed and he brought many bad men who threatened my friends. A good man and myself fought them and the bad men were killed and my friends were safe. After that I went back to explain to my chiefs what I had done and why. They understood and I was given an honourable discharge from the army. Every word I am saying to you is true, He-Dog, I swear to the white man's God. I swear on the life of all those I hold dear.'

Again there was a pause before He-Dog replied. 'I like what I hear you say, Captain, but I have liked the words of white men before. White men's words are like pretty flowers, they wither and die when the cold wind blows. Tell me why I should believe you. Tell me why I should take my braves into a white man's trap.'

John thought for a moment and then he stepped forward and this time he held out his hand. 'He-Dog can believe me because when He-Dog rides against the cavalry that attack the village I will be beside you. I will fight against the men who come to harm those men, women and children. Then you will see that what I have told you is true.'

After what seemed to John a long time but was probably only seconds, He-Dog reached out and shook his hand.

Josh and Charlotte sat miserably in the bar trying to decide what their next move was to be. Josh had a beer sitting untouched on the table before him and Charlotte's coffee was cold.

'Hell, he could be anywhere.' Josh shook his head helplessly.

Charlotte nodded glumly. 'If I had to guess I

would say he's gone back to that Indian contact, but I cannot for the life of me understand why. Have you contacted John's wife?'

'No, to tell you the truth I have no notion of what I am going to say to her. Knowing Connie like I do she is likely to go find that camp and drag that General fella out by his ears.'

Charlotte suddenly smiled. 'That's it.'

'What's it?'

'Let's save Connie the trip. I will be John's wife.'

'Say what?'

'I will go up there and be the enraged wife looking for her husband. I will drag General Fairweather out by his ears.'

Josh looked dubious. 'Sounds mighty dangerous to me.'

'Josh, this is what I am paid for.'

'I am riding up there with you.'

Charlotte shook her head. 'No you are not. You are staying here in the hope that John returns. Otherwise if he does come back he will simply ride off again to go back to camp to protect me, and to protect you and to protect any woodchuck or dung beetle that looks as though it might come to harm.'

Josh thought he was way too old to be taking instructions from this young woman but it was hard to fault the logic of what she was saying.

He smiled ruefully. 'Well I will say this, Charlotte, you sure as heck know John Carshalton.'

# CHAPTER NINE

John shivered slightly in the chill of the dawn, and then looked around guiltily lest any of the warriors around him thought he was shivering from fear. If any of them did they were not showing it. All were staring ahead, probably each man lost in his own thoughts as he waited for the fight to begin.

John was painfully aware that this was his first military engagement. He had fought and killed but never in an encounter like this. It scarcely compared to the great battles like Waterloo or those more recent that had slaughtered so many in the Civil War, but would be a battle for all that.

They were mounted, sitting just below the crest of a rise that hid them from the village. At the top of the crest lay a line of braves with bows at the ready. John had argued long into the night with Bristow trying to interpret what He-Dog was saying and explain at the same time.

'Indians do not do battle plans,' he explained to John, 'at least these Indians don't.'

'Then how do they know what to do?'

'They have a method. They like to break their enemy down, separate men from the main force, hunt them down. They do not take risks.'

John was exasperated. 'Well they cannot do that here. This is a cavalry charge. They will be close together. Even when they are approaching they will be bunched up. The kind of guerilla tactics you are describing just won't work. Wait until they are at full charge. We have the element of surprise. Get the archers. . . .'

'They won't know what an archer is.'

'The braves with bows then. Get them to fire into the cavalry. It will decimate them and cause confusion. Then we, the main force, will attack on their flank. They will try to turn to meet us head on and at that point we hit them.'

Eventually a plan of sorts had been agreed.

The village was now empty of all except some of He-Dog's warriors stationed there to take down any cavalry that made it that far. The occupants of the village had all been herded down to the river and there they sheltered under the protection of a few more of the warriors.

John looked back and saw Bristow sitting just behind He-Dog. The young man's pale skin seemed incongruous with the paint and the feathers. John felt incongruous himself, dressed as he was in his red British Army tunic. If he was going to die in battle, he reasoned, he would do it wearing the uniform of Her Imperial Majesty, and anyway it paid to be very visible to braves in the thick of the fight.

There was a rustle of bushes over to his left and a brave approached at a crouch and reported to He-Dog, who raised his war lance high in the air. John drew his sword slowly, letting it whisper out of the sheath.

'They are coming through the trees now,' Bristow hissed behind him.

John nodded and whispered back, 'Once they are clear of the trees they will sound the charge.' Bristow said something to He-Dog, who nodded grimly.

John felt his stomach tightening and a moment's panic spread over him. He had heard the tales of the way that fear can do anything to a man from loosening his bowels to freezing him to the spot. He forced himself to be calm. He patted Pilot's neck, worried that the animal was being affected by his sense of panic, although Pilot was a cavalry horse so was used to moments like this. John had won him from a fellow officer in a wager over cards and the man had hated him for it ever since.

The bugle sounded from just over the hill sooner than he had expected. He heard the pounding of hoofs together with a loud yell from the riders. At that the braves rose and for a moment the air in front of them seemed filled with arrows.

John heard no order to charge but as one the Indian warriors urged their horses forward. John was caught slightly unawares and urged Pilot on so as not be left behind.

The warriors who had fired the arrows scattered as the horsemen charged through. In a moment they were over the rise and pouring down on White's cavalry unit, which was already in disarray. A number of men and horses were already on the ground. Many of those still upright had both man and beast peppered with arrows. Those unhurt became aware of the Indians approaching. The warriors were emitting screams so piercing that they seemed to come from inside John's head. Then suddenly they were in amongst the blue-coated soldiers and the world around John consisted only of the man directly in front of him. He clashed his sword with one of the cavalrymen and felt the shock vibrate to his wrist; the other man raised his sword again. John pulled on the reins and Pilot obediently took a pace back. John thrust low with the sword, taking the man in the stomach; he screamed and went down. A pistol shot whistled past his ear and John wheeled the horse and drove in close to a man who was trying to bring his pistol to bear on John. John drove the hilt of the sword into the man's face, feeling bone and flesh crushing and tearing as he did. The man cried out and pitched forward. John slashed down with his sword as he fell.

John had heard old soldiers talk of the 'joy of battle' and he always had a certain scepticism for these stories. Now he was experiencing it for himself. All the fear had gone. Everything around him seemed to slow down. All around him warriors with hatchets, knives and clubs were grappling with soldiers with swords, pistols and rifles. The world was one of men screaming in pain and terror and rage. A rider charged him and John swung his horse away to let him pass, then hacked back with his sword, catching the man across the back of the neck. He then had to parry another blow from a dismounted soldier. He thrust downwards with his sword, which entered through the man's neck and out through his chest. With a grunt the man collapsed taking John, who was still holding the sword, out of his saddle to the ground.

John tried to pull the sword from the dead man's body but it was stuck fast. He had become separated from Pilot. Out of the corner of his eye he became aware of a soldier riding down on him, sword held high to cut downwards. John ripped his pistol from its holster and shot the rider in the chest. The man pitched backwards off his horse, and John caught the reins and let the momentum of the animal carry him into the saddle. The horse shied a little at the unfamiliar passenger but John soothed it and pulled it around to rejoin the fight.

Ahead of him he could see White.

John drove his unfamiliar horse forward but his way was blocked by fighting, struggling men. Through the chaos he saw White drag one of his own wounded men out of the saddle, holding him across his own body. For a moment John thought he must be witnessing a rare moment of bravery and compassion from the man, but he was wrong. White galloped towards a gap on the edge of the fighting where a young warrior was standing with a bow. As White rode at him the Indian fired arrow after arrow towards him but he was aiming at the man and not, as he should have done, at the horse. The body of the man White had dragged from his horse was riddled with arrows. White rode the Indian down, there was a scream and the boy went down under the hoofs of the horse. White let the body of his fellow soldier fall lifeless to the ground as he rode on back into the trees.

Again a dismounted soldier, probably more interested in getting a horse to ride out than to fight John, dragged him off the horse to the ground. The man raised his sword and John, with pistol still in hand, pulled the trigger only to hear the dull click of an empty gun. He realized he had no memory of firing that many times. As the sword came down he threw himself under the downward arc and crashed full force into the soldier, driving him to the ground. Before the other man could recover John reversed the pistol in his hand and using the butt as a club bludgeoned the soldier beneath him. Blood and brain sprayed into his face.

The next moment recall sounded and those soldiers still on horseback, of whom there were few, drove their horses out of the fight and back into the trees. Some of the warriors made to follow them but shouted orders from He-Dog brought them back.

Suddenly there was quiet save for the moans and cries of the wounded. John stood, hardly able to believe that it was all over. He began to shake slightly and felt a strong hand on his shoulder. He turned and found He-Dog standing beside him. The man studied him for a few moments and then nodded and moved on.

John stared around him. Dead men and horses lay everywhere, soldier and Indian. John wondered how long the fight had raged. It seemed like hours but probably had been over in fifteen or twenty minutes. John sought out Bristow, who was bleeding from a cut to his arm but seemed otherwise unhurt. He looked at John's face. 'Are you all right?'

John nodded, 'Somebody else's blood.'

He bent to one of the corpses and tore away the blue blouse to reveal the Confederate uniform underneath. 'Get He-Dog,' he said tersely and while the boy was away John exposed several more Confederate uniforms. The deception was undeniable.

He-Dog joined them and stared dispassionately at the evidence before him. After a while he spoke. 'He-Dog cannot deny what his own eyes can see. It is clear that Fairweather was trying to deceive us and was willing to destroy an innocent village. Such a man is not one that we can trust. We will not fight alongside General Fairweather. We will fight the white man when we are ready and where we want to. We will unite as one Indian nation to fight the white man and together we will drive them into the sea.' He turned to look straight at John. 'You were true to your word, Captain Carshalton, and you fought bravely and well, as you said you would. I believe you to be a man of honour. You will ride away from here in peace and safety, and you will always be welcome in He-Dog's lodge.'

The two men shook hands and He-Dog turned and walked away. John felt an immense relief. He had achieved what he had set out to do.

He became aware of several shots ringing out around the battlefield. 'What's that?' he asked Bristow.

'Some of the wounded soldiers are shooting themselves,' Bristow replied in a matter-of-fact-way.

'In God's name, why?'

'They do not want to be killed by the Indian. It is a slower death.'

John looked about him and everywhere corpses were being stripped naked. He was about to ask Bristow why this was happening when the mutilation of the corpses began. Some had numerous arrows fired into them, others had organs and extremities and private parts removed. Many were being scalped. The battlefield had come to resemble an abattoir.

'Dear God,' John exploded, 'this is obscene, inhuman.'

'It's their way.'

'It's barbaric.'

Bristow shook his head. 'When they killed my pa and captured me I expected a terrible death. Instead they took me into their world, taught me their ways. I listened to miners talk about what happened in the war so I guess we ain't so dainty either. These are ancient people with ancient ways and we have come in and destroyed their way of life.'

'But mutilating corpses, what is the point of that?'

'They are scared that their fallen enemy may try to seek revenge in the spirit world. So they try to prevent them by making them not able to fight.'

John looked around and shook his head, then he turned his attention back to Harry Bristow and saw an intelligent boy who as a child had been dragged into the filth and degradation of a mining camp and then had found peace in an ancient world so far from his own.

John sighed, 'Who knows?'

A brave had found Pilot and led him over to John. John shook hands with Bristow and swung into the saddle. Trying not to look at the battlefield, he trotted away.

Once clear of the village John turned Pilot east and headed for St Joseph.

# CHAPTER TEN

Charlotte drove the hired buggy hard up the trail towards the army camp. It bumped and twisted on the rough track but she kept the horses under tight control. Charlotte was a good horsewoman and she knew it.

Growing up as the youngest child with three older brothers, who were happy to tease her and pull her pigtails but less interested in letting her play in their games, she had to learn to ride and shoot and wrestle and climb the tallest trees, but most of all she had to learn not to cry. If she fell from the tree or the horse and the tears began to well up in her eyes she had learned to blink them back, wave her hand to show she was all right and race straight back to start again.

Her mother, who had longed for a little girl to put in pretty dresses and wear ribbons in her hair, despaired of a daughter who only wanted to get into her faded dungarees and battered straw hat that were her trademark. And when her mother died of the fever when Charlotte was twelve she had felt a dreadful guilt and sadness that she had not given that kind-hearted woman the pleasure in a daughter that she should have had.

However, that did not stop her when her brothers died, trying to join the army in any capacity, first to the amusement of the recruiting office and then to their exasperation as she came back time and again insisting that she would be happy just to march into battle without a rifle, beating the drum, she would assist the cook, she would help the doctors. But each time she was sent away.

A young lieutenant from the recruiting office was regaling a senior officer in the mess one night with the story of the crazy female who wanted to go to war. The senior officer was a major in army intelligence, the Bureau of Military Information, as it was then known.

Charlotte found herself recruited by the Bureau, initially as an administrator, which she hated, but in the fullness of time to work in the field. She worked in the South where she cultivated a peculiar Southern accent that she explained away as the result of having spent time in a fine school for young ladies in England. She learned quickly that her job was to smile prettily, gently stroke the arm of a Confederate officer and say in an awestruck voice, 'Why, Major, I declare, I wager you have plans to give those Yankee devils a real hiding.'

But now Charlotte intended to play an entirely different kind of female: the angry wife. And only part of the role needed her to act, as she was, without any doubt, angry.

She felt that Reynolds had mismanaged this whole problem from the outset. They had been facing a small force headed, as they now knew, by a weak delusional man. The US Army knew that it was happening in Missouri; people talked, and it would not have been hard to have tracked them down and dismantle the whole misguided operation. Instead Reynolds had dithered on the periphery, prevaricating over what action to take and had allowed this madman to open a dialogue with a race of people utterly disillusioned with the US Government and their empty promises; a race of people who did have the means to fight the US Army on a large scale at the expense of thousands of lives.

What really made her angry now, however, was the way in with John Carshalton had been emotionally blackmailed into becoming a part of this.

Firstly his involvement had been undersold and then his role stretched to the point where he was being put in harm's way. John, she quickly learned, had a heightened sense of honour and duty and found it hard to refuse Reynolds who to his mind still represented a superior officer. He had been forced to go and negotiate with the Indians, having no experience of this kind of work and with no knowledge of what Fairweather had promised. And now he was missing.

Charlotte rounded a bend in the trail and the familiar guard stepped out of the trees with his rifle half raised and hand held up. Charlotte cracked the whip over the heads of the horses and the buggy increased speed. Only at the last moment did the young soldier realize that she had no intention of stopping, and helped by Charlotte lashing the thick end of the whip over his upraised arms he tumbled into the undergrowth as she sped past and disappeared around another bend in the trail.

She drove the buggy uphill until the gates of the makeshift fort came into view and she was pleased to see that they were open. Despite shouted warnings from the soldiers on the walls she hurtled through the gates and pulled the horses to a halt in the middle of the small parade ground.

She was immediately surrounded by soldiers with their rifles raised. Sergeant Major Breeze stepped through the circle and stood in front of her.

'Climb down, please, miss.'

Charlotte scowled at him, 'Mrs. Mrs John Carshalton.'

One of the watching soldiers chuckled, 'Yeah, that figures.'

Breeze swung round, 'Shut your mouth.'

He asked again, politely but firmly, 'I have to

ask you to step down, Mrs. Carshalton.' He offered up his hand to help her down. She accepted and stepped down on to the dust of the parade ground.

She said, in a voice loud enough to carry, 'Where is my husband?'

'I am sorry, ma'am, the Captain is away for a couple of days.'

'And when are you expecting him to return?'

'I can't rightly say, ma'am.'

Charlotte drew herself up to her full height, which still only took her to Breeze's chest. 'Very well then, I want to speak with General Fairweather.'

All the time she was studying the camp trying to get a feeling for the size and military strength of the small army. She was also trying to think of her next move. What did John 'being away' mean?

Breeze was trying to maintain quiet dignity to the end. 'The General cannot be disturbed, Mrs Carshalton.'

'The General has already been disturbed.'

All eyes turned in the direction of Fairweather, who had left his tent and was walking towards the group around the buggy. The soldiers all snapped to attention and Breeze saluted.

Charlotte saw that Fairweather had only one leg and was surprised that John had not mentioned it, and then was puzzled as to why his leaving out that detail bothered her so much.

'Stand down,' Fairweather snapped and then to

Breeze, 'What in hell is going on here, Sergeant Major?'

'This is Captain Carshalton's wife, General. She wants to see him.'

'Well she damn well can't.'

Charlotte stepped in between them, causing both men to take a step back. 'I would thank you, General, not to speak about me as though I was not here and not to use profanity in my presence. I am simply asking where my husband is.'

Fairweather was struggling with his annoyance at the interruption and his duty to behave like a Southern gentleman.

'I regret to inform you, Mrs Carshalton, that Captain Carshalton is away at another camp and will not be back for a day or so.'

This did not make sense. What reason would John have to go to another of the camps? It had to be a ruse to be somewhere else, and if that was so it was obviously not to get back to St Joseph, therefore the only thing she could imagine was that John had returned to the Indian contact, but why?

'Very well, General, I demand that you send somebody to fetch him back this moment. It is imperative that I speak with him.'

Fairweather's patience deserted him. 'You "demand", madam? You are in no position to demand anything. You should not have been allowed access to this camp, and you should not have been allowed to see what you have seen.'

Charlotte was realizing that she might have over-played her hand. 'Very well, General, I will return to the town. I would be grateful if you could inform my husband that I will be there waiting for him.'

She turned to climb back into the buggy but Fairweather stepped forward. 'No, madam, you will not. If Captain Carshalton had a wife waiting for him in the town he neglected to mention it.'

He turned to Breeze, 'I want her taken and put in one of the tents under armed guard until Captain Carshalton returns to verify that she is who she says she is. And,' he pointed at the buggy, 'I want that damn thing off this army camp. Unhitch those horses and get that little girl's joyrider off this post.'

Charlotte watched in dismay as the horses were unhitched and the buggy pushed enthusiastically through the gates by a group of soldiers who, with a cheer, gave it an almighty shove that took it off the trail and crashing down through the trees where it eventually turned over and over, splintering as it went. That, Charlotte thought, is a bill that will not please Colonel Reynolds.

Charlotte tried bluster but she had little faith that it would do any good. 'This is an outrage, General. I have powerful friends . . .'

'And I, madam, have no need for powerful friends. When this is over I will be the most power-ful man in the Confederate States of America.'

At that moment Charlotte realized that John had

not exaggerated the madness of this man, and for one of the few times in her young life she felt afraid. She allowed herself to be led away by the soldiers without another word.

When Josh descended the stairs to the hotel lobby it was to find John relaxing in a soft leather chair sipping a cold beer and reading the local newspaper. He looked up in surprise as Josh approached him.

'Where the hell,' Josh thundered, 'have you been?'

John smiled. 'You really must practise these greetings, Josh. They appear to lack a certain warmth.'

Josh was in no mood for banter with his friend. 'Have you seen Charlotte?'

'Ah, you two have met. No, I was about to ask you the same question.'

'She went off looking for you.'

'Where?'

'Where? The Reb camp, where else? And I should have gone with her, 'cept she wanted me to stay here in case you turned up. Which you did.'

'And she has not returned?'

' 'pears not.'

'Then we need to ride there now, tonight. Agreed?'

'You'll get no argument from me, son.'

'Oh, by the by, why are you here?'

'I'll tell you later. Let's go and find Charlotte.'

*

Charlotte was sitting watching the night fall through the slight gap in the tent flaps. The tent itself was empty and she was forced to sit on the ground, with nothing to divert her apart from the food and water that had been brought to her late afternoon.

She had been allowed out of the tent to pee under the leering supervision of the young soldier guarding her. However, when rebuttoning her drawers she had taken her time in letting her skirts fall back into place, reasoning that, unpleasant prospect as it was, the young man's obvious interest in her might afford her a means of escape after darkness fell.

Fortunately, it was a method she was not forced to use, since at that moment White and what was left of the cavalry detail that had attacked the Indian village were just riding into camp, and everything was about to change.

White dismounted, looking both weary and afraid, as several of the survivors had to be helped off their horses and carried away. Fairweather having been advised of White's return immediately left his tent.

As he approached his warm smile of greeting quickly faded. 'In God's name, White, what happened here?'

'We got beat, General.'

'Got beat?' Fairweather was struggling to make sense of what he was hearing. 'How can you have? Where are my men?'

114

'Dead and scalped, most of 'em'

'But how? You had repeating rifles. Against a small village of non-combatants.'

White snorted, 'Non-combatants. We was ridden down by hundreds of braves, and that was after they had fired arrows in amongst us.' He felt that exaggeration was needed here.

'You mean they were ready for you?'

'Oh yes, they were ready for us all right. They were ready and waiting.'

'How could they have known?'

'Oh well now, that is an easy one to answer, General. Guess who was right up front there leading them on. That damned cut-throat rattlesnake Englishman.'

'Carshalton?'

'The same.'

Fairweather stood stunned for a moment, trying to digest this. 'Come to my tent, White. Now.'

He turned and made his way back to his tent with White following behind. Once inside Fairweather turned to White. 'Tell me what happened.'

'I've told you what happened, General. We waited 'til dawn like we agreed. We came down on 'em silent as cats. Next minute the air was full of arrows and then the next hundreds of screaming redskins come over the hill at us, and right up front with them was that stuck-up sonofabitch Englishman. I told you not to trust that no-good back-stabbing sneak, but would you listen to me?'

'That will do, White. You forget yourself, sir.'

'Sorry, General,' White was trying to calm himself and failing.

'We need cool heads here. We need to understand what this means.'

'It means we have been betrayed, General. It means the game's up. The injuns know it was us disguised as Yankees. It means they ain't going to fight for us.'

Fairweather was starting to shake with rage. 'Damn treachery, that's what it is, just damn treachery. Well, it's a setback, that's for sure.'

White could not believe what he was hearing, '"A setback"? Are you mad?'

'Hold your tongue, man. I will not be spoken to like that. Yes, it means we have to concentrate on building up our own forces to take on the North. It might take a year or two more.'

'A year or two.' White could not believe what he was hearing. 'Do you think we are going through another two years of this?'

'Well, what do you suggest?'

'I "suggest" that we stop playing at soldiers, pick a Yankee town full of banks and cattlemen and railroads and get in there, take all the money we can lay our hands on, burn it to the ground, and hightail it south as rich men.'

Fairweather stood staring at White, unable to take in what he was hearing.

'You want me to take this New Army of Northern

Virginia and use it to rob banks?'

White was reaching the end of his patience. 'You damned fool, do you really think you are going to whup the Yanks with this bunch of kids and old men? Let's just make ourselves rich and get the hell out of here.'

Fairweather shook his head. 'My God, that is all you have ever wanted, isn't it? You just want to line your pockets. You have never believed in this cause. You are right, how can I ever achieve anything when I have scum like you as my second in command? You are nothing but a rogue and a cut-throat, a petty little sneak thief. I doubt that you have ever held a commission in your life, you liar. God help me, for all his treachery, Carshalton was a soldier. If I had had a military man leading the attack on that village he would have prevailed. Instead I had a low-life cowardly piece of vermin like you. Get out of my sight. Get out of this camp and do not come back. You are not fit to spend your time amongst soldiers.'

White had had enough. He had been through what was, by anybody's standards, a bad day. He had tolerated this delusional fool when he thought it would make him rich; now he saw all of that slipping away from him and he was simply not prepared to let that happen.

With an almost weary detachment he took his revolver from the holster where it had remained all throughout the fight with the Indians, pointed it between the eyes of a startled Fairweather and pulled the trigger. With that single shot White finished the proud line of the family of warriors that were the Fairweathers. It ended there, to nobody's great alarm.

The force of the shot drove the General back out of the tent and left him spread-eagled on the ground.

Charlotte heard the gunshot and the shouts of alarm that followed. She peered out of the flaps of her tent at the back of her guard, who was on his feet staring in the direction of the shot.

Another soldier came running towards them. 'He's shot him. Captain White has shot the General.'

Her guard shook his head. 'The hell you say?'

'Go see for yourself if you don't believe me. He's lying outside his tent shot clean between the eyes.'

The guard took the other man's advice and set off across the parade ground. Charlotte stepped outside the tent into the chill night air. Keeping to the edge of the camp in the deeper darkness she worked her way around the perimeter until she came to the paddock where her horses were tethered. She pondered her next move.

She could see no saddle that she could steal and she did not rate her chances trying to ride bareback. Her horses were a team and if she could find something for them to pull she might still get away.

She cast about until she could make out a wagon in the darkness. It was a while since she had set up a

118

team to a wagon as well as having to work in the darkness but eventually the horses were in harness and ready to go. She climbed up to the seat and started moving the wagon gently forward. She would have liked to have skirted the perimeter again but tents and wooden storage containers blocked her way and she was forced to move slightly more into the light of the campfires as she approached the gate.

The camp seemed in turmoil as she moved quietly by. People were running and shouting. Loud arguments were breaking out. She could hear Breeze trying to restore calm. She moved out through the gates that still stood open having let White and the few survivors of the Indian fight enter. There were no guards on the walls. She moved out through the gates and into the darkness. She waited for a shout or a bullet to come her way but then she was moving, gathering speed as she went down the trail.

The guard, however, was in his usual position and as she failed to heed his shout to stop he raised his rifle. She tried to lie sideways on the wooden seat while still controlling the team of horses. Shots rang out behind her and then she was swallowed by the darkness again and she was on her way.

Only now the alarm had been raised. If men were sent after her they would probably head towards Miller's Crossing, where she had claimed to be staying, so as the trail divided she turned the opposite way, west towards Kansas.

That decision proved crucial as thirty minutes later John and Josh rode through Miller's Crossing and took the trail up to the camp.

# CHAPTER ELEVEN

Breeze stood over the body of the General looking shocked and disorientated. White himself seemed to be coming to terms with what had happened.

Breeze spoke first, 'What have you done?' and then to answer his own question, 'You've killed the General.'

'He was going to give up.'

'Why?'

'We've lost the Indians.'

'Lost the. . . .' Breeze trailed off, then, 'Then I guess he was right to give up.'

White had never at his best been a quick thinker and after a day such as this his mind certainly did not feel nimble. However, he realized that whatever riches he had promised himself and the tight little band that followed him were about to vanish if the New Army of Northern Virginia decided to call it a day.

'So you never believed in the cause, then?'

This startled Breeze somewhat; he had never seen White as anything other than in this for himself.

'Of course I believed in it, why the hell would I have gone this far if I didn't? But without the Indians we do not have the firepower to take on the whole Yankee army.'

'Then we don't take on the whole Yankee army. We hit them hard, we hurt them, then we vanish. I learned how to do that when I rode with Quantrill.'

Breeze doubted very much that White had ever ridden with Quantrill but was past caring. 'We have already done that.'

'I don't mean make some noise and burn a few barns, I mean hit hard. I mean we hit a major town. We hit it with artillery, and infantry and horses. We hit somewhere which will hurt them in the pocket. Somewhere that will have politicians running for cover from the money men who bankroll them.'

'Somewhere in mind?'

'Abilene.'

'Hell.'

'Cattle town, major rail depot,' and with enough banks and businesses with big safes to keep me for the rest of my life, White thought greedily. Breeze stood rubbing his chin trying to think this through. Finally he made a decision.

'I'll go along with this, Captain White, but I will say this to you and you would do well to heed it. I do not trust you, sir,' he had to force the last word out. 'We've got brave boys out there who believe in what they are doing and they are prepared to die to make the South great again, to bring back the way of life we all fought for. If you let those boys down, if you lead them into hell and leave them there, then you had better hope that I die there too, 'cause if I make it out I will hunt you down if takes the rest of my life, and I will kill you.'

White relaxed a little; he had Breeze on his side, at least for the time being. 'Noted, Sergeant Major. Now I would thank you to show your new commanding officer some respect.'

At that moment one of the sergeants burst into the tent. 'Sorry to disturb, Captain, Sergeant Major, but Captain Carshalton's wife has gone.'

White swung round on him. 'Captain Carshalton's wife?'

'Yes, Captain. Sorry, sir, you wouldn't know Captain Carshalton's wife rode in earlier today demanding to see him. The General put her under armed guard.'

'And now she's gone.'

'So, let the bitch go.'

'She's taken the wagon with the repeating rifles in, sir. You see we smashed up her buggy, sir, on the General's orders.'

White cursed heavily and loudly, 'Get a detail together and go and get those guns back.'

'Yes, sir. What do we do with the Captain's wife, sir?'

'Kill her – I don't give a damn.'

'Kill the Captain's wife?'

'Just do it, damn you.'

The sergeant fled. Breeze turned a puzzled gaze on White. 'Not sure Captain Carshalton will take kindly to you killing his wife, not to mention you just automatically assuming command.'

White carefully, and with his own exaggerated detail of his own courage and leadership, told Breeze the story of Captain Carshalton's cowardly treachery.

'Don't worry, Breeze, you will not be hearing from Captain Carshalton again.'

John and Josh eased their horses slowly up the trail to the army camp until they were near the bend where John knew a guard would be posted.

'Stay here,' he hissed to Josh. 'They know me. I will get us past the guard.'

Josh dismounted and led his horse into the trees. John moved forward around the bend and duly the sentry stepped out to stop him. In the darkness John was almost on to him before he recognized him.

'Captain Carshalton, sir. We didn't think we would be seeing you again, sir.'

John was not surprised by this. He suspected White would have returned by now and would have told Fairweather his story.

'Well,' he said pleasantly, 'now you have seen me. So I will just get on up to the camp.'

The sentry raised his rifle. 'I'm sorry, sir, I have been told you are not to pass. That I have to hold you here.'

'What's this about, soldier? What's going on?'

'I can't tell you that, sir.'

At that moment Josh appeared behind the young Confederate, wrapped a strong forearm around his neck and held a knife in front of his face. The rifle fell from the terrified soldier's grasp. Josh turned him round and pressed him back up against a tree.

'Do you know what happened the day Jackson surrendered, boy? I'll tell you. I sat down on a log and wept like a little girl. Do you know why, boy?' The terrified lad shook his head. 'I'll tell you. It was 'cause I loved killing Rebs and for the last six years I have missed killing Rebs something hurtful. And then suddenly here you are, another Reb for me to kill after all this time. So you just tell the Captain whatever it is he wants to know before I decide to get my hand in agin.'

The boy was grateful to be able to look at John instead of Josh. 'All hell's broken loose up there, sir. Captain White has killed the General and he's taken command.'

'My God.' This John had not expected.

'Word is we are getting ready to march, sir.'

'March where?'

'Don't rightly know, sir, west I've been told. Oh and your wife has gone, sir.'

For a moment John was confused, 'My wife?' Then it dawned on him. It must have been Charlotte. It would have been a sensible story for her to tell to get entry to the camp.

'Yes, sir, the General had her under armed guard, sir, but she must have got out when there was all the uproar about the General being shot. And she took a wagon, sir, 'cause the boys had smashed up her buggy. On the General's orders, sir.'

'Where has she gone?'

'I wouldn't know, sir, she came past me like a bat out of hell. And Captain White, he sent Sergeant Dixon and a detail to fetch the wagon back, sir.'

'How long ago?'

'About an hour ago.'

John looked at Josh. 'We need to get after her, fast.'

Josh released the guard from the tree, took his rifle and with one swing broke it against the tree. 'Now git, son, before I take up Reb killing again.'

The boy scampered off, not up the trail as good sense might suggest but back into the woods.

Josh sighed, 'Fine to say get after her, but which way has she gone?'

'West. If she had gone through the town we would have met up with her. We need to find her before White's men do. I doubt if anyone is in any mood to show mercy to women at the moment and certainly not one that claims to be *my* wife.'

As the light in the sky behind her slowly became brighter, Charlotte pulled the horses to a halt next to a small stream. The horses were tired and shaking from their exertions, more so than Charlotte had expected, but then the wagon felt heavy to handle.

She looked behind her and saw a large load covered with a heavy sheet. She climbed over the box seat and pulled back the cover to reveal large wooden boxes. With difficulty she heaved one of the boxes over the side of the wagon and let it smash open against a rock.

Out spilled about twenty Henry repeating rifles. Charlotte realized to her dismay that her random choice of transport had turned out to be something that the new Confederate army would not want to lose.

Up until now she had decided that once she put enough distance between her and the camp any pursuers would give up and go back, but for a wagonload of repeating rifles that was unlikely. She might have gained some time by going west, but it would not have taken long for whoever was following to realize their mistake and turn around.

She looked at the horses and realized that they were in no fit shape to continue for a while, not unless she wanted to kill them. She realized that she would probably have to stay and fight. She could simply hand the wagon back to them but in the turmoil after the death of Fairweather it was likely that the chasing soldiers would not be in a merciful mood.

She searched in the wagon and found some smaller boxes that contained the special cartridges needed for the guns. She broke one of these open with the butt of a rifle and loaded sixteen cartridges into the breech, levered one into the chamber and loaded a seventeenth.

She got the complaining horses to move the wagon closer to a cluster of large rocks, then unhitched them and led them away from the wagon.

Almost on cue she could hear the clatter of hoofs and knew that those chasing her were arriving. Her instinct was to move as far away from the wagonload of guns and ammunition as possible but she also reasoned that the soldiers might be more careful with their shooting if they did not want damage done to the precious cargo. She hunkered down behind the rocks. She had about a hundred cartridges and a good rifle. This was about as good as it was going to get.

The riders came around the bend. There were probably about fifteen Confederate soldiers and they were at full gallop. She knew it would take a few moments for them to register that the wagon was stationary on the trail, and she had to use that moment. She rose from behind the rocks and fired quickly, levering and firing, levering and firing. The riders were still moving fast so were harder to hit, but as she fired one man pitched out of the saddle and another collapsed screaming over his horse's neck. Another's hands flew to his head, blood streaming down his face.

For a few moments all was turmoil, and Charlotte used those moments to drop back behind the rocks and reload.

Sergeant Dixon was an experienced NCO and he quickly restored order, getting his men dismounted and into whatever cover they could find. In the short time since they had rounded the bend Dixon had two men dead and another bleeding profusely from a head wound.

His first response was to establish where the shooter was, but that quickly became obvious and he was not happy with the knowledge.

'Take care, boys,' he shouted. 'It's coming from behind the wagon and there's live rounds in there.'

He did not relish telling White that they had blown up, or at least severely damaged, his consignment of repeating rifles.

'Spread out,' he shouted. 'See if you can work your way around behind.'

Charlotte heard this from her shelter and her heart sank. It was going to be hard to defend her back on her own, but she had little choice other than to try. She was firing more carefully now, trying to pick her targets.

A man broke cover trying to get across to her left. She tracked him and fired. He screamed and went down. She found that the position behind the rocks was restricting her. She rolled forward, cursing the dress she was wearing, which was wrapping round her legs and restricting her movement. She was now almost under the wagon.

There was a shout from in front of her, presumably

passing on the information that she had moved. A man rose from cover to take aim and she aimed and fired and he went down without a sound.

She was scanning around waiting for somebody else to move. Several shots were coming her way now as the soldiers spread out and the earth in front of her was being kicked up. Then she became aware of somebody above her. She rolled on to her back and saw one of the soldiers on the box seat raising his rifle to take aim. She tried to swing her own rifle up but in her haste it caught against one of the wheels of the wagon. The soldier smiled as he raised the rifle, then his expression changed to one of surprise. The rifle dropped from his hands and he fell forward across the boxes of guns.

For a moment Charlotte thought he must have been shot by one of his own companions but that did not seem likely. She realized somebody else must have joined the fight.

John and Josh could hear the sound of gunfire as they approached and as they rounded the bend they quickly saw what was happening.

'Get to higher ground,' John shouted, and they were both off their horses and climbing the steep slope, with John in front and Josh panting behind. As they came to the top of the rise John threw himself down and Josh did the same.

'There,' Josh shouted, pointing, and John looked in time to see the Confederate soldier jump on to the box seat of the wagon. He took careful aim and fired, watching the man fall across the guns where his body twitched a few times and was still.

Dixon had seen his man fall and assumed that the girl had shot him, but suddenly shots were coming in from somewhere above them. Another man screamed and rolled out from the rock he had been crouching behind. Shots were coming in from two different directions and another man went down. Dixon knew he had been outflanked. 'Pull back, boys,' he shouted. 'Let's get out of here.'

The wrath of White and Breeze was preferable to being shot to death. The soldiers ran to their horses, hauled into the saddle and galloped back down the trail.

Charlotte watched them go and crawled out from under the wagon and stood up. She was covered in dust, bleeding from a cut from a flying rock chipping; she felt a dishevelled mess.

She watched John and Josh make their way down the slope. To her annoyance she was beginning to shake slightly. She had killed men before but she never got used to it. As John approached she fought a desire to rush into his arms and seek comfort. Instead she just smiled and said, 'Well, you two took your own good time getting here.'

They found the team of horses and hitched them to the wagon. The dead soldiers they laid together by the rocks. They had no means to bury them and would have to leave them to the mercy of the buzzards and the creatures of the night.

Charlotte climbed back onto the wagon and the two men sat on their horses on either side.

'Where to now?' Josh asked.

John sighed, 'I suppose we should head back to St Joseph and report to Colonel Reynolds.'

'Hmm,' from Charlotte. 'You might want to rethink that?'

'Why?'

'Did Josh not tell you why he came to St Joes?'

John suddenly remembered, 'No Josh, you never did tell me.'

Josh grinned. 'Well it's like this, son. God in his wisdom has decided that we need to have another Carshalton in the world. My feeling is we already have enough, but there you go.'

John sat looking blank. Charlotte leaned forward and put her hand on his shoulder.

'John, you are going to be a father.'

'Well I guess that means we're going to Arabella.' Josh turned to grin at his friend but John was already several hundred yards down the trail.

# CHAPTER TWELVE

'What you have to understand,' Colonel Reynolds was saying, 'is just how stretched we are.'

The 'we' was the US Army and on this Reynolds did not exaggerate. They had been short of the required strength since the end of the war. The Indian wars and the need to police the South had stretched them further. The last thing he needed was a madman leading a lost cause taking them to the brink of another Indian war.

And now he had been reliably informed that the rebels were on the move.

'Do we know where they are going?' John asked.

They were sitting in Declan's office; Reynolds, John, Josh, Charlotte and Declan.

Reynolds sighed, 'They are heading into Kansas, that's for sure. At the request of the Governor we have garrisoned troops in Abilene and Wichita. We have to protect the business interests there.'

'Speaking of business interests,' Declan interrupted, 'we have a few here.'

The Colonel looked apologetic. 'I appreciate that, Mr Finn, but it is a matter of scale.'

Josh spoke for the first time. 'It is a matter of a lot of innocent people who need protection as much as cattle bosses and railroad owners.'

'I appreciate that, Josh, but I only have so many men. My advice to all the smaller towns would be to evacuate as many folks as will go to the cities. Then we can protect them. In any case if we understand their motives correctly they mean to disrupt business and commerce, and that will make places like Abilene a prime target.'

John frowned. 'Let us be sure we do understand their motives. Fairweather was a delusional madman who wanted to rerun the Civil War with a different outcome. Now the phony General has been replaced by a phony Captain. White is a cut-throat thief and coward who is in this only to line his own pockets and escape south before the inevitable defeat.'

'Then why are they following him?'

John shook his head, 'That is harder to understand. Sergeant Major Breeze is a professional soldier and in my view a decent man. White must have persuaded him that they could still achieve what Fairweather set out to do.' He thought for a moment. 'Where are they now?'

'Camped on the border.'

'And an attack is not feasible?'

'It is, but not without significant loss of life.'

John decided. 'I need to talk with Breeze.'

Josh grabbed him by the arm. 'Are you crazy? White will kill you.'

'Not if I go in under a flag of truce.'

'White does not strike me as the type who is going to take notice of a white flag.'

'No, but Breeze will.'

Reynolds looked uneasy. He had already had the rough edge of Charlotte's tongue for the danger that he had put the Englishman in the way of and he did not want his name on sending John into further trouble. 'Let me send one of my best officers. Better still, I will go myself.'

'I appreciate that, Colonel, but it has to be me. I got to know Breeze a little while we were together and he is more likely to listen to me than someone who, if you will forgive me, he will see as a damned Yankee.'

There was a pause while everybody tried to think of a way out of this.

Josh shook his head. 'You're mad, John. How the hell are you going to tell Connie?'

'Are you mad?' Connie was on her feet in their living room, her fists clenched, screaming up at him.

John reached out to rest consoling hands on her shoulders, 'Connie, calm yourself. Think of your condition.'

'I am thinking of my condition. I am pregnant and I would rather like my child to meet their father.'

'Connie, you are being hysterical.'

'Don't,' screamed Connie, on the verge of hysteria, 'tell me I am being hysterical.'

'But you are, notwithstanding.'

'That's because you make me hysterical.' Connie realized she had just defeated her own argument at a stroke.

'It is just to talk.'

'Oh yes? It's like "gathering information" means getting involved in battles and shoot-outs over wagons full of rifles?'

She sat down and burst into tears. She was immediately furious with herself for crying but it seemed the only thing to do. She remembered the relief she had felt the day before when two riders had approached down Main Street escorting a wagon driven by what Connie could tell, even through the dust and the blood, was a very attractive young woman.

Connie had almost dragged John from his horse in her eagerness to hug him. When she had finally released him her first words were a terse 'Who is she?' indicating Charlotte.

'My mistress,' John had informed her. 'It is expected of all English gentlemen that they keep a mistress and a wife both.'

At that Connie had punched him hard on the

arm, thought about it and punched him again.

'Ow!'

'That is just in case you ever think that might be a good idea.'

However, she had taken Charlotte over to the hotel and used Declan's patronage to get her a good room. When Charlotte had appeared bathed and changed they had sat in the lobby of the hotel and taken tea together. Inevitably they had talked about John.

'You and John seem to have worked together very well.' Connie was fishing and Charlotte knew it. She had taken Connie's hand.

'Connie, I would like us to be friends, so let me say this at once. I will not say that I was not at all attracted to John. He is very handsome and very charming. He is also one of the most married men I have ever met. He is a one-woman man and you are that woman.'

Connie had gratefully squeezed Charlotte's hand and they had sat and chattered happily.

Now John sat beside her and put his arm around her as she cried.

'I am going to try and stop more bloodshed. I trust the soldier I am going to see. He will not harm me. Whether he will listen to me remains to be seen. I can only try, and having tried I will be back here and you will have my complete and undivided attention. That I promise you. You must trust me on this, Connie. I am the only one who can do this.'

She dried her eyes and looked firmly at him. 'John, it is always you. You cannot take on all the ills of the world. How America survived before you came along to save it is a mystery to me.' She sighed. 'Very well, this last time, and then your world will be us and our unborn child. Go, I will wait for you as I always do.'

Sergeant Major Breeze was dreaming of home, of his parents' small farm in Georgia, and of their one family of slaves: husband, wife and son. He and the son, Elijah, had grown up together and had been the dearest friends. Every Thanksgiving and Christmas the slaves would join Breeze and his parents for dinner. Then in '62 Elijah had gone to fight for the North. He had fallen at Antietam and Breeze remembered his mother and Elijah's mother receiving the news and clinging to one another weeping. That night Breeze's father had gone to old Abel and said, 'You're free now, Abe. Your boy done earned that for you. You are a free man. You can go where you will.'

The slave had sucked on his old clay pipe and smiled softly at the farmer. 'Heck, Mr Breeze, reckon we've always been free. You is way too good a folks to send hounds after another man. You is kind people and there ain't too much kindness around just now. So if it is OK with you I would like to carry on working beside you each day and sitting here on my own porch of an evening and think of all the good times with young Elijah.'

Breeze had never once seen his father cry but had seen how hard the man was fighting to keep the tears back as he had squeezed the black man on the shoulder and turned and walked away.

Breeze awoke with his own tears streaming down his face and became aware of someone shouting his name. He angrily pushed the tears back with the heel of his hand and climbed out of his cot.

Sergeant Dixon burst into his tent. 'Captain Carshalton is coming in, Sergeant Major. He has a white flag.'

As Breeze left the tent White came storming across. 'Dixon, why is that sonofabitch still alive? Shoot him off that horse, and the old fool he's got with him.'

Dixon looked dismayed. 'But he's under a white flag, sir?'

'I don't give a good damn what rag he's waving around – kill him.'

Breeze stepped forward. 'You will not. He has come here to parley and that is what he is going to do.'

White was beside himself with rage. 'Damn you, Breeze, I will have you shot for this. Just who the hell do you think you are? Have you forgotten who you are talking to?'

Breeze had had enough. Something inside him gave way. He turned to face White.

'I haven't forgotten who you are or what you are.

I know who I'm not talking to. I'm not talking to a captain, I'm not even talking to a soldier. I am talking to a low-life piece of scum that is only here to line his pocket. "Who do I think I am?" I think I am the man who is taking charge. I am relieving you of duty, Captain,' he spat the last word, then turned to Dixon. 'Arrest this piece of trash and keep it under armed guard, and let Captain Carshalton through.'

As John and Josh rode into the camp Breeze was standing waiting for them. 'Best you and your friend climb down, Captain, I ain't getting a stiff neck trying to talk up to yer.'

They sat on felled trees to talk. John looked about him. 'Where's White?'

'Captain White has been relieved of his command.'

'I cannot tell you how it gladdens my heart to hear that.'

'What have you come to say to us, Captain?'

'Simply that I want you to stop this now. I want you to disband and send these men home before they all travel home in pine boxes.'

'That sounds like a threat, sir.'

'It isn't. It is a plea from the heart, Sergeant Major. The US Army has men in every major town and city in Kansas. If you go to another state the same thing will happen. You are a good soldier, Breeze. Too good to let men die for no reason.'

'Sir, when we joined General Fairweather, hell we

140

knew he wasn't no General but he had a plan and we thought his heart was in the right place.'

'His heart may have been but his head was not.'

'Well, we didn't necessarily understand that straight away. But we joined up to hit back at the North, hit back at the no-good chancers who are all over our lands like termites. We fought a hard war just like the North and we deserve better than we got. So, you don't give up the cause just because your senior officer is gone.'

'You do if the cause is lost, and it is. Look, Breeze, I am English, this was not my war and I did not have to fight in it, but Josh here did.'

Josh leaned forward to look Breeze in the eye. 'We fought in different colour uniforms. We fought for different things, but I will tell you this – whenever we came together every Reb I came up against was as scared as I was, all of us just trying not to soil ourselves. Every Reb fought as hard as me. Everyone wanted to win as much as I did, and every one of them wanted to go home as much as I did. We aren't going to see eye to eye on things for a long time, maybe never. But hell, son, we both saw things no man should ever have to see. Enough is enough now, let these boys go home.'

It was easily one of the longest speeches John had ever heard Josh make and he could see it had a profound effect on the rebel soldier. His shoulders seemed to sag and a great weariness came over him. It seemed to John as though the man aged in front of his eyes.

Breeze sat on the tree for what seemed ages, lost in his thoughts, then he looked up at John and Josh. 'Guess it ends here then.'

John felt an enormous relief wash over him, and for the first time he was conscious of the strain of the last few days.

They became aware of a soldier running through the trees calling out to Breeze. The soldier had a black eye and was bleeding from a cut on his head. He stopped in front of Breeze.

'I was guarding Captain White, Sergeant Major, and they jumped me.'

'Who jumped you?'

'White's friends, that crowd he hangs around with. They carried me about a mile from the camp and then dumped me.' He turned to John. 'They sent a message to you, sir.'

'To me?'

'Yes, sir. White said he knows a little town near Abilene has a bank just right for the taking. He said to tell you, sir, he's going through that mother and burn it to the ground.'

John and Josh exchanged worried glances and with quick handshakes with Breeze they were on their horses and riding away from the camp.

Breeze watched them go and then shouted to the men around him, 'OK, break camp.'

One of the soldiers shouted enthusiastically, 'Where are we heading, Sergeant Major?'

Breeze looked west into the vastness that was Kansas and at the two riders quickly becoming smaller in the distance.

'Home, son. We're going home.'

# CHAPTER THIRTEEN

Declan sat on the porch of his hotel and watched his customers return from their buffalo hunt.

They were the three young Englishmen that John had clashed with a couple of weeks before. Declan knew them as Gerald, Frederick and Thomas. The only reminder of their meeting with the sheriff of Arabella was that Gerald's natural good looks were marred by a kink in the nose that John had broken.

With their Sharps Model 1874 50-calibre rifles slung over their shoulders they chattered happily as they climbed down from the converted wagon that had taken them out on to the Great Plains, where they had been able to shoot at the huge running beasts. Declan knew that in the back of the wagon would be a large pile of buffalo hides for him to sell at a profit.

He greeted the Englishmen warmly and chivvied his staff to get baths ready for the three men. This done, he returned to the porch to take his ease. After a very short while the hunting party left the hotel and headed over the street to the saloon, although on this occasion they were careful not to take any firearms with them.

A little later Charlotte stepped out of the hotel and stood gazing out of town. Declan approached her and raised his hat.

'A very good afternoon to you, miss. You will be looking for our dashing young sheriff, I'll be bound.'

Charlotte turned a chilly gaze on Declan. 'Just taking the air, Mr Finn, just taking the air.'

'Of course, miss, I did not mean to imply anything untoward, him being the happily married man as he is.'

'Yes, he is, is he not? And you Mr Finn, any woman catch your eye or are you already married to your money?'

'You do me a disservice, miss. It is just that I have failed to attract a woman who can see the real person in me.'

'Mr Finn, I find that very hard to believe.'

She turned back to watching the far horizon and then stiffened slightly. 'Mr Finn, are you expecting one of your hunting parties back?'

'One arrived back a short a while ago, three Englishmen, they over in the saloon.'

'Nothing bigger expected?'

'Not for a week or so.'

Charlotte frowned. 'Then I think we have trouble coming.'

Declan joined her in staring out. He too could see what was obviously a number of riders coming at some speed.

Charlotte spoke sharply, 'Get as many people off the street as you can.'

She turned and ran back into the hotel and up to her room. She quickly stripped off her dress and petticoats and pulled on a pair of breeches and a shirt.

She rushed back down and out of the hotel. She ran across the street, which was being hurriedly cleared of people, to the sheriff's office. She burst in and grabbed up several keys on a large ring. She cursed as she struggled to find the key to the gun cabinet.

Once it was open she strapped on a gun belt and holster and slid a pistol into the holster. She loaded the rifle and the pistol, then grabbed extra shells for the rifle and dashed outside. She looked up and down the street trying to decide the best position to engage with the horsemen, whom she could now see clearly, still coming at a gallop. She decided that one of the bedrooms at the nearer corner of the hotel would serve best.

She dashed back over Main Street and into the hotel, up the stairs and along the passage to the room she had identified. She burst open the door to find an elderly man sitting smoking a cigar and reading *Homer's Odyssey*.

'Get down on the floor,' she shouted at him.

146

He looked at her with an indulgent smile, 'My dear child, if I get down there it is unlikely I will get up again.'

'Mister, if you don't get down, it is a certainty you won't get up again because nasty men with big guns are going to blow the living hell out of this room on account that I will have just killed a couple of them.'

It surprised Charlotte just how fast an elderly man could get under a bed. She raised her rifle and waited.

White was feeling better than he had felt for many weeks. Playing soldiers had never suited him. The military gave the world fools like Fairweather and hard-asses like Breeze. Now he felt free, surrounded by men driven by the same need for wealth and lack of any moral constraints in how that wealth was achieved. He had before him a town without any law, without the army and with a nice fat bank doing a nice trade. He felt good.

It was a slight disappointment then to burst into the town shooting and uttering rebel yells to have the man to his left scream as a bullet hit him in the chest and plucked him back off his horse.

Several other shots followed and two more men went down, one clearly dead, the other clutching his stomach and crying with pain.

'He's up in that hotel window,' someone shouted.

'Blow him out of there,' White snarled. 'Brady, you come with me to the bank.'

Hugging the side of the street closest to the hotel

147

and therefore narrowing the angle of fire for whoever was in the corner room, White and Brady drove hard down the street. Behind them several of White's men were concentrating fire on the corner room while others were trying back alleys to work their way around the other side.

In the hotel room shots began to shatter glass, take down pictures and part of the ceiling. Charlotte decided it was time to move and left at speed. As more debris flew and the very woodwork began to disintegrate, a bony hand crept out from under the bed, grabbed *Homer's Odyssey* and pulled it to safety.

Over in the saloon the three Englishmen were sipping beers and congratulating each other on their successful hunt when the sound of shooting, first a single rifle and then a number of guns, broke through their shouted conversation. All three dashed to the window.

'I say, you fellows, some rotters are shooting up the place. That's not playing the game when chaps just want to have a quiet beer.'

Gerald called across to Sam, who also understood what was happening outside and was busy pulling his shotgun out from under the bar, 'I say, my man. Would you happen to have any confiscated weapons behind that bar?'

'Help yourself,' was Sam's gruff retort. The three men ran behind the bar and pulled out some repeating rifles.

'Any spare ammo?' Frederick asked.

'Do I look like a gunsmith?'

'Well,' said Gerald, looking at the collection of firearms under the bar, 'from this angle you do rather.'

All three grabbed rifles, crossed to the window and beat out the glass with the weapons' butts, which Frederick conceded later was a touch unnecessary as the window opened on hinges, but 'we got a bit carried away.'

With limited ammunition the three men had to pick their targets, which they successfully did as two men went down and another staggered away holding his arm. Sam had also joined them and his shotgun blasted out across the street.

'Who are these wretched people anyway?' Frederick enquired as he fired the last shot in his rifle and had the satisfaction of seeing one of the men fall forward out of sight.

'No idea, old thing,' Gerald responded, 'but they do not strike one as gentlemen.'

Charlotte rushed down the stairs to the lobby, crossed to the door and eased it open, expecting to attract fire from the men who had been shooting at the hotel, but was confused to see that they were now firing at the saloon from which she could see the barrels of rifles sticking out through broken glass.

She was planning her next move when a pistol was placed against her head and a voice said, 'Drop

149

that gun, little girl, before you hurt somebody.'

She turned to find a man with a toothless grin pointing his gun straight at her head. Then Declan's voice came from her right. 'No, friend, you drop yours before you get hurt.'

They both spun round to see Declan pointing a double-barrelled shotgun at the man's midriff. The man swung his pistol away from Charlotte to bring it to bear on Declan, but before he could manage that both barrels of the shotgun fired, the force of which carried the man back through the window of the hotel and out on to the sidewalk in a storm of broken glass.

Declan was about to speak when another shot was fired. Declan cried out and went down clutching his leg. A second man was standing framed in the doorway that led to the kitchen but he had made the mistake of concentrating on the man with the now empty weapon, not the person with the loaded rifle. Charlotte levered and fired three times. The man crumpled over a table which flipped and came down on him. He lay still underneath it.

Charlotte turned back to Declan, whose leg was bleeding heavily. 'Let me help.' She moved forward but Declan waved her away. 'Get to the telegraph office. Tell Abilene we are under attack.'

Charlotte still had time to be sarcastic, 'Really? I was just going to tell them it's started to cloud up here.'

Declan snarled, 'Give me a bad time later, just get

to the telegraph office.'

Charlotte broke out of the hotel at a run. Bullets chewed up the woodwork around her and as she reached the general store she felt the need to take some cover. She burst in through the door of the now empty shop and threw herself to the floor as the window exploded and glass showered down on her.

Across the street the three Englishmen had seen Charlotte's rush down the sidewalk.

'I say,' Gerald commented, 'that chap's attracting a bit of fire.'

'Sure it was chap, old boy?' Frederick demurred. 'He had awfully long hair.'

'I say, this is no time to be commenting on a chap's appearance.'

'Well, I was just saying.'

'Look,' Gerald decided, 'I'm going to give him a hand. Give me some cover would you, there's good fellows.'

With that he was out of the door and running across the street as his two companions pumped shots at the small group of men still crouching near the hotel. Gerald was still obliged to weave as he ran since some shots were coming from the top of the buildings behind him.

Charlotte saw him coming and assumed at first he was one of the bandits, but it was obvious that he was attracting fire, and he seemed to have come from the saloon where she had seen shots directed at the invaders earlier. She took a chance and kicked open the door. Gerald saw it open and dived gratefully through to land on some sacks of flour which over-balanced and carried him to the floor. He sat up, dusting himself down.

'I say, that was bracing.'

'Ah,' light dawned for Charlotte, 'you must be one of Declan's hunting party.'

'The very same. I say, Freddie was right. You are a girl.'

The side door of the store flew open and a man dived in, firing as he went. Charlotte had her pistol in her hand in a moment and placed three bullets in the man before he could take aim.

'I say, you do shoot jolly well.'

'For a girl?'

A man appeared in the doorway and Gerald coolly raised his rifle and shot him the chest. The man grunted, spun away and lay face down on the sidewalk.

'For anyone.' He gazed at her admiringly.

'Cover me,' Charlotte told him. 'I have to get to the telegraph office.'

'Of course, my pleasure. I say, I don't suppose you would do a fellow the honour of having dinner with me this evening?'

Mad, Charlotte thought as she sprinted out of the door, the English are all stark raving mad.

As she moved at a crouching run down the side-walk she could see horses outside the bank and knew what was happening. This was White getting what he had wanted all the time, she thought bitterly, and of course he would pick Arabella, the ultimate revenge on John Carshalton.

She ducked down an alley to avoid the fire and ran as a man appeared ahead of her. She still had her pistol in her hand and fired as she went. He went down and she jumped over him, not even bothering to look and see if he was dead.

She had lost all track of time or the people she had shot. She had never been in a battle but she thought this must be what it was like, no reality, no point of reference.

She reached the telegraph office and bundled inside. Old Clem Orton was crouched on the floor and she nearly fell over him.

'I've sent it, miss,' in response to her urgent request. 'I got it out quickly before these vermin pulled the wires down but I gave 'em credit for more sense than they've got. I've had the chance to telegraph the numbers and what they're after.'

'The bank,' Charlotte said grimly.

In the bank, White had watched Brady place the dynamite and the fuses. He much preferred to be in the bank than outside where bullets were flying. Several more men had arrived at the bank with empty saddle-bags ready to take away as much money as the gang could manage. The fuses were set and everybody moved outside.

Thus it was as John and Josh galloped into town

every window in the bank blew outwards at once, causing both horses to shy and in Josh's case deposit him cursing onto the ground. At once bullets kicked up the dirt around him from men crouched on the roofs of the saloon and adjoining buildings. Josh sought shelter behind a horse trough and started to return fire.

John brought Pilot under control and galloped as close as he could to the buildings on his right from where fire was being directed. John wanted White and he knew exactly where he would be.

Josh was trying to draw a bead on the men on the roof but he had only a pistol, his rifle still tucked in its sheath on the side of his horse. Suddenly there was the breaking of glass from the hotel immediately behind him and the boom of a hunting rifle. One of the shooters cried out and pitched forward, sliding down the roof to fall silently into the street.

Frederick had decided there was little more he could do from the saloon and had sprinted across to the hotel. He got his beloved Sharps from under the bed. He had knocked the window out – something he was beginning to enjoy – and taken the man on the roof.

He called down to Josh, who was still trying to return fire from behind the horse trough, 'I say, you there, do come up and join me. It is a better angle and altogether safer.'

Josh dragged himself from behind the trough and ran as quickly as he was able into the hotel, and promptly fell over Declan, who was trying to keep the flow of blood from his wounded leg to a minimum.

Declan screamed in pain and Josh raised an apologetic hand as he went up the stairs at a depressingly pedestrian pace.

John approached the bank as a man came out carrying heavy saddle-bags. On seeing John he dropped the bags and drew his gun. John already had his in his hand and fired three times from his horse. The man staggered, clutched at his chest and tripped over the saddle-bags to pitch forward down the steps of the bank and lie still in the dust.

John dismounted, slapped Pilot on the rump to get him away from the gunfire and then ran up the steps to flatten himself against the wall just outside the door. Bullets splintered the wooden frame and he dropped to the wooden boards and rolled in to the bank.

The main area was still smoky from the dynamite and the door of the big safe hung on one hinge. White and Brady were busy filling saddle-bags with money and another man was already coming towards John.

John fired twice and the man fell clutching his side and groaning in pain. White, seeing John, ran to his left and crashed through the door to the manager's office. Brady drew his gun and fired, the bullet creasing across the lower part of John's neck, causing blood to flow down his front and tears of pain to fill his eyes.

He threw himself sideways, trying to clear his head and his eyes. Brady fired again and missed as John came up firing. Two bullets took Brady in the chest and a third caught him in the throat. He fell backwards into the safe and slid to the floor with banknotes raining down on him.

John saw White pass the window, heading away from the bank and towards the small house that stood a short distance away; John's house, where he knew Connie would be.

Josh and Frederick had cleared the roofs opposite. Two more men had dropped into the street before at last the remainder of the gang who were, as Frederick remarked, clearly not deep thinkers, decided enough was enough, and jumped on their horses and headed out of town.

Connie had been unsure what to do when she heard the shooting start. She had thought of seeking shelter in the hotel but that would probably take her into harm's way so she had decided to stay where she was, which had seemed the right decision until the door was kicked open and White stood on the threshold. He was about to enter when a shout from behind made him turn around. John was advancing on him from the bank with the pistol pointed straight at his chest.

'Just make one move and I will kill you,' John informed him as he approached.

White made to step back into the house and John

knew he had no choice. He pulled the trigger and heard the dull click of an empty revolver. In his haste he had forgotten to reload.

A broad smile spread over White's face. 'Well, well, Captain, what a dumb thing to have done for such a clever guy.' He came down the step from the house to confront John. 'Well, I guess I get to settle a score after all.'

Connie, standing behind White, could see what was about to happen and to do nothing was not in her nature. Just outside the door lay a scythe that, in a rare moment of domesticity John had used to clear some scrub from around the front of the house. She picked it up and stepping forward drove it as hard as she could manage between White's shoulder blades.

White cried out and turned to face Connie with the scythe still sticking in his back. He raised the gun to shoot Connie; John was helplessly already moving forward but he knew he could not make the distance to reach White in time.

Then a shot rang out. White staggered and turned. As he did two more shots punched holes in his chest. He stood for a moment looking bewildered and then his legs buckled and he dropped to his knees, clawing at his shirt to try and see the wounds, and then with a soft moan fell sideways and lay still.

John turned to his right to see Charlotte standing with the rifle still at her shoulder. 'I think,' she said quietly, 'that will do for today.'

And indeed it did.

The remainder of the gang had ridden away empty-handed and a few hours later a company of US Cavalry arrived.

'Good of yer to turn up,' was Josh's unhelpful comment.

The veteran sergeant riding behind the captain surveyed the street and whistled. 'It's been a while since I've seen this many dead Rebs. Makes me pine for the old days.' His captain scowled at him.

The three Englishmen were standing gazing around, and Gerald wrapped his arm around Josh's shoulder as one does to a comrade with whom you have just come through a battle. 'I say you fellows,' Gerald enthused, 'that was jolly exciting, wasn't it?'

The sergeant looked at Josh and rolled his eyes. Josh shrugged, 'Don't tell me, son, we have an English sheriff.'

The sergeant nodded as though that explained all.

The captain leaned down to Josh, 'Which way did they go?' Josh jerked his thumb south and the company were wheeled around and headed off, leaving a small contingent and most importantly an army surgeon whose first task was to try and save Declan's leg.

This he managed to do but there had been much blood loss and some muscle damage, which meant that Declan would probably walk with a stick for the rest of his life.

As White lay dead Connie rushed into John's arms sobbing and then gave a small cry when she saw the blood down the front of his blouse, but it was quickly traced to the crease of the bullet on his neck.

When Charlotte approached them Connie hugged her as well. 'Think this is bad,' Charlotte said philosophically, 'I have a dinner date with a crazy Englishman.'

Connie nodded sympathetically, 'I don't think there is any other kind.'

And gradually the town started to return to normal and repair the damage both physical and psychological. As one of the townsfolk drily put it, 'If we didn't have a shoot-out at least once a year we wouldn't know this was Arabella.'

White's gang were chased over the border but had scattered. It was decided that pursuit was not worthwhile.

The army camp was taken over by the US Cavalry and a large number of arms and artillery were recovered.

Some recruits of the New Army of Northern Virginia were caught and detained, including Sergeant Major Breeze, but it was generally felt that the last thing that was needed at the moment were martyrs and they were eventually freed and allowed to return home.

Charlotte was roundly praised by Colonel

Reynolds for her part in bringing the business to a close, but as she was female no medals were forthcoming. As one Washington visionary put it, 'Damned females are already clucking about getting the vote, it would not do to encourage them further.'

The next day John and Josh sat on the porch sharing a jug and watching the sun go down.

'Josh,' said John firmly, 'this is all I want. A wife who is better than I deserve. . . .'

'Amen to that.'

John ignored him, '. . . and a good friend to share a jug with. From here on in I fully intend to learn to be content with what I have. If I ever suggest I am going to get involved in anything other than the job I am paid to do, I give you permission to shoot me.'

Josh rose from his chair and started towards the office.

'Where are you going?'

Josh smiled, 'To get my rifle, son, it will save time.'